William Gifford

The Baviad and Maeviad

William Gifford

The Baviad and Maeviad

ISBN/EAN: 9783337397456

Printed in Europe, USA, Canada, Australia, Japan

Cover: Foto ©Andreas Hilbeck / pixelio.de

More available books at **www.hansebooks.com**

THE

BAVIAD,

AND

M Æ V I A D,

BY

WILLIAM GIFFORD, Efq.

———————

Tota cohors tamen eft inimica, omnefque manipli
Confenfu magno officiunt, curabitis, ut fit
Vindicta gravior quam injuria : dignum erit ergo
Declamatoris Mutinenfis corde Vagellî
Cum duo crura habeas offendere tot caligatos.

———————

A NEW EDITION REVISED.

———————

LONDON:

PRINTED FOR J. WRIGHT, OPPOSITE OLD BOND
STREET, PICCADILLY.

———————

MDCCXCVII.

INTRODUCTION.

In 1785, a few Englifh of both fexes*, whom chance had jumbled together at Florence, took a fancy to while away their time in fcribbling high-flown panegyrics on themfelves ; and complimentary "canzonnettas" on two or three Italianst, who underftood too little of the language

* Among whom I find the names of Mrs. Piozzi, Mr. Greathead, Mr. Merry, Mr. Parfons, &c.

† Mrs. Piozzi has fince publifhed a work on what fhe is pleafed to call BRITISH SYNONIMES; the better, I fuppofe, to enable thefe gentlemen to comprehend her multifarious erudition.

a 3

in which they were written, to be difgufted with them. In this there was not much harm ; nor, indeed, much good : but, as folly is progreffive, they foon wrought themfelves into an opinion that they really deferved the fine things which were mutually faid and fung of each other.

Though " no one better knows his own houfe" than I the vanity of this woman; yet the idea of her undertaking fuch a work had never entered my head; and I was thunderftruck when I firft faw it announced. To execute it with any tolerable degree of fuccefs, required a rare combination of talents, among the leaft of which may be numbered neatnefs of ftyle, acutenefs of perception, and a more than common accuracy of difcrimination ; and Mrs. Piozzi brought to the tafk, a jargon long fince become proverbial for its vulgarity, an utter incapability of defining a fingle term in the language, and juft as much Latin from a child's Syntax, as fufficed to expofe the ignorance fhe fo anxioufly labours to conceal. " If fuch a one be fit to write on SYNONIMES, fpeak." Pignotti himfelf laughs in his fleeve; and his countrymen, long fince undeceived, prize the lady's talents at their true worth,

Et centum Tales* curto centuffe licentur.

* Quere Thrales ?   PRINTER'S DEVIL.

Thus perfuaded, they were unwilling their inimitable productions fhould be confined to the little circle that produced them; they therefore. tranfmitted them hither; and, as their friends were enjoined not to fhew them, they were firft handed about the town with great affiduity, and then fent to the prefs.

A fhort time before the period we fpeak of, a knot of fantastic coxcombs had fet up a daily paper called the WORLD *. It was perfectly unintelligible, and therefore much read: it was equally lavifh of praife and abufe, (praife of what appeared in its own columns, and abufe of every thing that appeared elfewhere,) and as its conductors were at once ignorant and conceited, they took upon them to direct the taste of the

---

* In this paper were given the earlieft fpecimens of thofe unqualified, and audacious attacks on all private character; which the town firft fmiled at for their quaintnefs, then tolerated for their abfurdity; and now—that other papers equally wicked, and more intelligible, have ventured to imitate it, —will have to lament to the laft hour of Britifh liberty.

town, by prefixing a fhort panegyric to every trifle which came before them.

It is fcarcely neceffary to obferve that Yendas and Laura Marias, and Tony Pafquins, have long claimed a prefcriptive right to infeft moft periodical publications : but as the Editors of them never pretended to criticife their harmlefs productions, they were merely read, laughed at, and forgotten. A paper, therefore, that introduced their trafh with hyperbolical encomiums, and called on the town to admire it, was an acquifition of the utmoft importance to thefe poor people, and naturally became the grand depofitory of their lucubrations.

At this aufpicious period the firft cargo of poetry arrived from Florence, and was given to the public though the medium of this favoured paper. There was a fpecious brilliancy in thefe exotics, which dazzled the native grubs, who had fcarce ever ventured beyond a fheep, and a crook, and a rofe-tree grove, with an oftentatious difplay of " blue hills," and " crafhing torrents," and " petrifying funs !"* From admiration to imitation is but a ftep. Honeft Yenda tried his hand at a defcriptive ode, and fucceeded beyond his hopes ; Anna Matilda followed; in a word.

———— contagio labem

Hanc dedit in plures, ficut grex totus in agris

Unius fcabie cadit, et porrigine porci.

✦ Here Mr. Parfons is pleafed to advance his farthing rufh-light. " Crafhing torrents and petrifying funs are extremely ridiculous"— *babes confitentem !* " but they are not to be found in the Florence Mifcellany." Who faid they were ? But àpropos of the Florence Mifcellany. Mr. Parfons fays I obtained a copy of it by a breach of confidence; and feems to fancy, good man ! that I derived fome prodigious advantage from it: yet I had written both the poems, and all the notes fave one, before I knew there was fuch a treafure in exiftence. He might have feen, if paffion had not rendered him as blind as a mill-horfe, that I conftantly allude to poems publifhed feparately in the periodical fheets of the day, and afterwards collected with great parade by Bell and others. I never looked into the Florence Mifcellany but once ; and the only ufe I then made of it, was to extract a founding paffage from the odes of that deep-mouthed Theban, Bertie Greathead, Efqr.

While the epidemic malady was fpreading from fool to fool, Della Crufca came over, and immediately announced himfelf by a fonnet to Love. Anna Matilda wrote an incomparable piece of nonfenfe in praife of it; and the two " great luminaries of the age," as Mr. Bell calls them, fell defperately in love* with each other.

* The termination of this " everlafting" attachment was curious. When the genuine enthufiafm of the correfpondence (Preface to the Album) had con-tinued for fome time, Della Crufca became impatient for a fight of his beloved, and Anna, in evil hour, confented to become vifible. What was the confe-quence !

Tacta places, audita places, *fi non videare*
Tota places, neutro *fi videare* places.

Mr. Bell, however, tells the ftory another way; and he is probably right. According to him, " Chance alone procured him an interview." What-ever procured it, all the lovers of " true poetry", with Mrs. Piozzi at their head, expected wonders from it. The flame that burnt with fuch ardour, while the lady was yet unfeen, they hoped would blaze with unexampled brightnefs at the fight of the bewitching object. Such were their hopes. But what, as Dr. Johnfon gravely afks, are the hopes of man ! or indeed of woman !—for this fatal meeting

From that period not a day paffed without an amatory epiftle fraught with lightning and thunder, et quicquid habent telorum armamentaria cœli.——The fever turned to a frenzy : Laura Maria, Carlos, Orlando, Adelaide, and a thoufand other namelefs names caught the infeftion ; and from one end of the kingdom* to the other, all was nonfenfe and Della Crufca.

put an end to the whole. Except a marvellous dithyrambic which Della Crufca wrote while the impreffion was yet warm upon him, and which confequently gave a moft accurate account of it ; nothing has fince appeared to the honour of Anna Matilda : and the " tenth mufe," the " angel," the " goddefs," has funk into an old woman ; with the comforting refleftion of having lifped love ftrains to an ungrateful fwain.

—— non hic eft fermo pudicus
In *vetula,* quoties lafcivum intervenit illud
Ζωη και Ψυχη.

* Kingdom. This is a trifle. Heaven itfelf, if we may believe Mrs. Robinfon, took part in the general infatuation.

" —— When midft etherial fire
Thou ftrik'ft thy DELLA CRUSCAN lyre,

Even THEN, I waited with a patience which I can better account for, than excufe, for fome one (abler than myfelf) to ftep forth to correct the growing depravity of the public tafte, and check the inundation of abfurdity that was burfting upon us from a thoufand fprings. As no one appeared, and as the evil grew every day more alarming (for now bed-ridden old women, and girls at their famplers, began to rave) I determined, without much confidence of fuccefs, to try what could be effected by my feeble powers ; and accordingly wrote the Following Poem.

    Round to catch the *heavenly* fong,
    Myriads of *wondering* feraphs throng !"

I almoft fhudder while I quote : but fo it ever is,

    Fools rufh in where angels fear to tread.

And Merry had given an example of impious temerity, which this wretched woman was but too eager to imitate.

THE

BAVIAD.

BAVIAD,

A

PARAPHRASTIC IMITATION

OF THE

FIRST SATIRE OF PERSIUS.

Impune ergo mihi recitaverit ille SONETTAS,
Hic ELEGOS!

P. WHEN I look round on man, and find
how vain
His paffions—
   F. Save us from this canting ftrain!
Why, who will read it?

PERS. SAT. I.

O CURAS hominum! O quantum eft in
rebus inane!
Quis leget hæc? Min' tu iftud ais? Nemo,
hercule. Nemo?

B

P. Say'ft thou THIS to me ?

F. None, by my life.

P. What, none ? Nay, two or three—

F. No, no ; not one. 'Tis fad ; but—

P. Sad ; but—Why ? 5

Pity is infult here. I care not, I,

Vel duo, vel nemo: turpe et miferabile. Quare ?

NOTES.

* *Cui non dictus Hylas ?* And who has not heard of
James Bofwell, Efq. ? All the world knows (for all
the world has it under his own hand) that this great
man compofed a BALLAD in honour of Mr. Pitt,
with very little affiftance from Trufler, and lefs from
Mr. Dibdin ; which he produced to the utter confu-
fion of the Foxites, and fung at the Lord Mayor's
table. This important " ftate paper" I have not
been able to procure, thanks to the *fcombri, et quicquid inepti amicitur chartis*, out the terror and dif-
may it occafioned amongft the enemy, with a variety
of other circumftances highly neceffary to be known,
may be gathered from the following letter :

To the CONDUCTOR *of the* WORLD.

SIR,

THE wafps of oppofition have been very
bufy with my *State Ballad,* " the GROCER of

ᵇ Tho' * Bofwell, of a fong and fupper vain,

And Bell's whole choir (an ever-jingling train),

ᵇ Ne mihi Polydamas & Troiades Labeonem

Prætulerint: nugæ.

NOTES;

LONDON;" and they are welcome. Pray let them know that I am vain of a hafty compofition which has procured me large draughts of that popular applaufe in which I delight. Let me add, that there was certainly no *fervility* on my part; for I publicly declared in Guildhall, between the *encores*, " that this fame " Grocer had treated ME arrogantly and ungratefully ; " but that, from his great merit as a Minifter, I was " compelled to fupport him !"

The time WILL come, when I fhall have a proper opportunity to fhew, that in one inftance at leaft, the man has wanted wifdom.

Atqui vultus erat multa & præclara minantis.

Poor Bozzy! But I too threaten.—And is there need of thy example, then, to convince me that on

———our firmeft refolutions
The noifelefs and inaudible foot of death
Steals like a thief!

B 2

In fplay-foot madrigals their pow'rs combine,
To praife * Miles Andrews' verfe, and cenfure
mine—   10
' No, not a jot.   Let the befotted town
Beftow as fafhion prompts the laurel crown ;

' ——Non, fi quid turbida Roma
Elevet, accedas : examenve improbum in illa

* This gentleman, who has long been known as an
induftrious paragraph-grinder to the morning papers,
took it into his head fome time fince to try his hand
at a Prologue.   Having none of the ufual requifites
for this bufinefs, he laboured to little purpofe ; till
Dulnefs, whofe attention to her childreu is truly ma-
ternal, fuggefted to him that unmeaning ribaldry and
vulgarity might poffibly be fubftituted for harmony, fpirit, tafte, and fenfe.—He caught at the hint, made the
experiment, and fucceeded to a miracle.   Since that
period every play-wright, from O'Keeffe to· Della
Crufca, " a heavy declenfion !" has been folicitous to
preface his labours with a few lines of his manufac-
turing, to excite and perpetuate the good humour of
his audience.   As the reader may probably not diflike a fhort fpecimen of Mr. Andrews's wondei-
working poetry, I have fubjoined the following ex-

But do not THOU, who mak'ft a fair pretence

To that beft boon of Heaven, COMMON SENSE,

Caftiges trutina : nec te quæfiveris extra.

NOTES.

tract from his laft and beft performance, his prologue
to Lorenzo.

    " Feg, cries fat Madam Dump, from Wap-
        ping Wall,
    " I dont love plays no longer not at all,
    " They're now fo vulgar, and begin fo foon,
    " None but low people dines till afternoon ;
    " Then they mean fummot, and the like o' that,
    " And its impoffible to fit and chat.
    " Give me the uppero, where folks come fo
        grand in,
    " And nobody need have no underftanding.

    " Ambizione ! del tiranno !
    " Piu forte, piu piano, a che fin—
    " Zounds ! here's my warrant, and I will come in.
    " Diavolo ! who comes here to fo confound us ?
    " The conftables, to take you to the round-
        houfe.
    " De round-houfe, ?—Mi !
    " Now comes the dance, the demi charactere,
    " Chacone, the pas de deux, the here, the there ;

B 3

Refign thy judgment to the rout, and pay   15
Knee-worſhip to the idol of the day:
For all are——

Nam Romæ eſt quis non ? ᵈ at, ſi fas dicere :
    ſed fas

"·And laſt, the chief high-bounding on the
    loofe toe,
Or pois'd like any Mercury, O che guſto !

And this was heard with applauſe ! And this was
read with delight ! O ſhame ! where is thy bluſh ?

——morantur
Pauci ridiculum effugientem ex urbe pudorem.*

* It is rightly obferved by Solomon that you may
bray a fool in a mortar without making him wifer.
Upon this principle I account for the ſtationary ſtu-
pidity of Mr. Andrews; whofe faculties, God help
the while! do not feem a whit improved by the
dreadful pounding he has received. Of him therefore I waſh my hands—but I would fain aſk Meſſrs.
Morton and Reynolds (the worthy followers of
O'Keeffe, and the prefent fupporters of the Britiſh

F. What? Speak freely ; let me know.

P. ᵈ O might I ! durſt I ! Then——but let
it go.

ᴿ

Tunc, cum ad canitiem, et noſtrum iſtud vivere
trifte

Afpexi, et nucibus facimus quæcunque reliais,

Cum fapimus patruos: tunc, tunc. Ignofcite. Nolo.

NOTES.

Stage) whether it be abfolutely neceffary to introduce
their Pieces with fuch ineffable nonfenfe as this

——Betty, it's come into my head
Old maids grow crofs becaufe their cats are dead ;
My governefs hath been in fuch a fufs
About the death of our old tabby pufs.
She wears black ſtockings—ha ! ha ! what a pother,
'Caufe one old cat's in mourning for another *!

If ɪᴛ ʙᴇ ɴᴏᴛ—for common-fenfe' fake, Gentlemen fpare us the difgrace of it ; and O Heavens ! ɪF
ɪᴛ ʙᴇ—deign in mercy fometimes to apply to the
Bellman, or the Grave-ſtone cutter, that we may ſtand
a little chance of having our ribaldry and our doggrel " with a difference."

* See ᴛʜᴇ ᴡɪʟʟ—A Bartholomew-fair farce by
Mr. Reynolds.

B 4

Yet, when I view the follies that engage

The full-grown children of this piping age;   20

See fnivelling Jerningham at fifty weep

O'er love-lorn oxen and deferted fheep;

See Cowley * frifk it to one ding-dong chime,

And weekly cuckold her poor fpoufe in rhyme;

See Thrale's grey widow with a fatchel roam, 25

And bring in pomp laborious nothings home;

See Robinfon forget her ftate, and move

On crutches tow'rds the grave, to † " Light o'

    Love;"

NOTES,

* For the *poetic* amours of this lady, fee the Britifh
Album, particularly the poem called the INTERVIEW;
of which, foit dit en paffant, I have a moft delectable
tale to tell, when time fhall ferve.

† Light o' Love, that's a tune that goes *without* a
burden.   SHAKESPEARE.

‡ In the firft editions of this and the following
poem, I had overlooked Mr. Parfons, though an un-
doubted Bavian. This nettled him. Ha! quoth he,
in the words of a well known writer, " Better be
damn'd than mentioned not at all." He accordingly

See Parſons ‡ while all ſound advice he ſcorns,
Miſtake two ſoft excreſcences for horns ;   30

NOTES.

applied to me* (in a circuitous manner I confeſs) and
as a particular favour was finally admitted, in the
ſhape of a motto, into the title page of the Mæviad.
Theſe were the lines.

> May he who hates not CRUSCA's *ſober* verſe,
> Love MERRY's *drunken* profe, ſo ſmooth and
>   terſe ;
> The ſame may rake for ſenſe in PARSON's ſkull,
> And ſhear his hogs, poor fool! and milk his
>   bull.

The firſt diſtich contains what Mr. Burke calls " high
matter ;" and can only be underſtood by the initiated ;
the ſecond (would it had never been written!) inſtead
of gratifying the ambition of Mr. Parſons, as I
fondly expected, and quieting him for ever, had a
moſt fatal effect upon his poor head, and from an ho-
neſt pains-taking gentleman converted him in ima-
gination into a Minotaur.

> Continuo implevit falſis mugitibus urbem,
> Et ſæpe in lævi quæſivit CORNUA frontem.

---

* PARSONS I know, and this I heard him ſay,
Whilſt Gifford's harmleſs page before him lay,
I too can LAUGH, I was the FIRST BEGINNER.
                    PARSONS of HIMSELF, Teleg. March 19.
Quam multi faciunt quod Eros, ſed lumine ſicco,
Pis major lachrymas RIDET, et intus habet!

And butting all he meets, with aukward pains,
Lay bare his forehead, and expofe his brains :
I fcarce can rule my fpleen ——

NOTES.

The Motto appeared on a Wednefday ; and on the
Saturday after, the morofoph Efte (who appears to
have believed in the reality of the metamorphofis)
publifhed the firft bellowings of Mr. Parfons, with
the following introduction :

On Mr. GIFFORD's MOTTO.

" The following SPIRITED CHASTISEMENT of
the vulgar ignorance and malignity in queftion, was
fent on Thurfday night—but by an accidental error
in one of our clerks, or in the fervant delivering
the copy at the office, it was unfortunately miflaid !"

Why, this is as it fhould be ;—" the Gods take care
of Cato !" Who fees not that they interfered, and
by conveying the copy out of the compofitor's way,
procured the Author of the Mæviad two comfor-
table nights ! But to the " fpirited chaftifement."

" Nor wool the pig, nor milk the bull produces."

The profundity of the laft obfervation, by the
bye, proves Mr. Parfons to be an accurate obferver
of nature : and if the three Irifhmen who went nine
miles to fuck a bull, and came back a-dry, had
fortunately had the honour of his acquaintance, we

F. Forbear, forbear:

And what the great delight in learn to fpare.

NOTES.

fhould probably have heard nothing of their far-
famed expedition.

" Nor wool the pig, nor milk the bull produces,
" Yet each has fomething for far different ufes :
" For boars, pardie! have tufks, and bulls have
" HORNS."

Η, Νεμεσις δε κακαν εγραψατο ΦΩΝΑΝ.

for from that hour fcarce a week, or indeed a
day, elapfed, in which Mr. Parfons did not make
himfelf ridiculous, by threatening me in the Telegraph, the Oracle, &c. with thofe formidable non-
entities.

Well and wifely fingeth the poet :—*Non unus mentes
agitat furor.* Yet while I give an involuntary fmile
to the oddity of Mr. Parfons' difeafe, I cannot but
lament that his friends (and a gentleman who is faid
to belong to more clubs than Sir Watkin Lewis,
muft needs have friends) I cannot, I fay, but lament that on the firft appearance of thofe knobs,
thofe " excrefcences, "as I call them, his friends did
not have him cut for the fimples!

‘ *P.* It muſt not, cannot be ; for I was
    born   35
To brand obtruſive ignorance with ſcorn ;
On bloated pedantry to pour my rage,
And hiſs prepoſterous fuſtian from the ſtage.
Lo, DELLA CRUSCA*! in his cloſet pent,
He toils to give the crude conception vent.   40

‘ Quid faciam ? ſed ſum petulanti ſplene cachinno.
Scribimus incluſi, numeros ille, hic pede liber,

NOTES.

* Lo, DELLA CRUSCA!

“ O thou, to whom ſuperior worth's allied,
“ Thy Country's honour, and the Muſes pride—”

So ſays Laura Maria—

            et ſolem quis dicere falſum
        Audeat ?

Indeed ſhe ſays a great deal more ; but as I do not
underſtand it, I forbear to lengthen my quotation.
Innumerable Odes, Sonnets, &c. publiſhed from
time to time in the papers, have juſtly procured this
gentleman the reputation of the firſt poet of the age :
but the performance which called forth the high-
ſounding panegyric above mentioned, is a philoſo-

Abortive thoughts that right and wrong confound,
Truth facrific'd to letters, fenfe to found ;

Grande aliquid, quod pulmo animæ prælargus
anhelet :

NOTES.

phical rhapfody on the French Revolution, called the
Wreath of Liberty.

Of this poem no reader *(provided he can read)* is
at this time ignorant: but as there are various opinions concerning it, and as I do not choofe perhaps
to difpute with a lady of Mrs R—'s critical abilities,
I fhall feleƐt a few paffages from it, and leave the
world to judge how truly its author can be faid
to be

        " gifted with the facred lyre,
  " Whofe founds can more than mortal thoughts
    infpire."

This fupernatural effort of genius, then, is chiefly
diftinguifhed by three very prominent features.—
1. Downright nonfenfe. 2. Downright frigidity.
3. Downright doggrel.—Of each of thefe in its turn :
and firft of the firft.

    Hang o'er his eye the goffamery tear.
    Wreath round her airy harp the tim'rous joy.
    A web-work of defpair, a mafs of woes.
    And o'er my lids the fcalding tumour roll.

Falfe glare, incongruous images, combine;
And noife and nonfenfe clatter through the line.

NOTES.

" TUMOUR, a morbid fwelling." JOHNSON. An
excellent thing to roll over an eye, efpecially if it
liappen to be hot and hot, as in the prefent cafe.

————fummer-tints begemm'd the fcene.
And filky ocean flept in gloffy green.

While air's nocturnal ghoft, in paly fhroud,
Glances with griefly glare from cloud to cloud.

And gauzy zephyrs, fluttring o'er the plain,
On twilight's bofom drop their filmy rain.

Unus inftar omnium! This couplet ftaggered me.
I fhould be loth to be found correcting a madman;
and yet mere folly feems unequal to the production
of fuch exquifite nonfenfe.

2do.

————days of old
Their perifh'd, proudeft, pageantry unfold.

————nothing I defcry.
But the bare boaft of barren heraldry.

————the huntrefs queen,
Showers her fhafts of filver o'er the fcene.

To thefe add, moody monarchs, radiant rivers,
cooling cataracts, lazy loires (of which, by the bye,

' 'Tis done. Her houſe the generous Piozzi
lends, 45

Et natalitia tandem cum ſardonyche albus,

there are none), gay garonnes, gloomy glaſs, mingling
murder, dauntleſs day, lettered lightnings, delicious
dilatings, ſinking ſorrows, rich reaſonings, melio‑
rating mercies, dewy vapours damp that ſweep the
ſilent ſwamp ; and a world of others, to be found in
the compaſs of half a dozen pages.

3tio.
In phoſphor blaze of genealogic line.
N. B. Written to " the turning of a brazen candle
ſtick."

O better were it ever to be loſt
In black negation's ſea, than reach the coaſt.

This couplet may be placed to advantage under the
firſt head.

Should the zeal of parliament be empty words.
——turn to France, and ſee
Four million men in arms for liberty.
——doom for a breath
A hundred reaſoning hecatombs to death.

And thither fummons her blue-ftocking friends;
The fummons her blue-ftocking friends obey,
Lur'd by the love of Poetry—and Tea.
The BARD fteps forth in birth-day fplendour
    dreft,
His right hand graceful waving o'er his breaft ; 50
His left extending, fo that all might fee,
A roll infcrib'd " THE WREATH OF LI-
    BERTY."

———————————

Sede legens celfa, liquido cum plafmate guttur
Mobile collueris, patranti fractus ocello,

NOTES.

A hecatomb is a facrifice of a hundred head of
oxen. Where did this gentleman hear of their *rea-
foning?*

    Awhile I'll ruminate on time and fate ;
    And the moft probable event of things——

EUGE, MAGNE POETA ! Well may Laura Maria
fay,

    That GENIUS glows in every claffic line,
    And NATURE dictates——every thing that's
    thine.

So forth he steps, and with complacent air,
Bows round the circle, and assumes the chair:
With lemonade he gargles first his throat,   55
Then sweetly preludes to the liquid note:
ᵍ And now 'tis silence all. GENIUS OR MUSE*—
Thus while the flowry subject he pursues,
A wild delirium round th' assembly flies;
Unusual lustre shoots from Emma's eyes;   60
Luxurious Arno drivels as he stands;
And Anna frisks, and Laura claps her hands.

ᵍ Hic neque more probo videas, neque voce serena
Ingentes trepidare Titos, cum carmina lumbum

NOTES.

* GENIUS OR MUSE, whoe'er thou art, whose
    thrill
Exalts the fancy, and inflames the will,
Bids o'er the heart sublime sensation roll,
And wakes ecstatic fervour in the soul.

See the commencement of the Wreath of Liberty,
where our great poet, with a dexterity peculiar to
himself, has contrived to fill several quarto pages
without a single idea.

C

[h] O wretched man ! And dost thou toil to
  pleafe,

At this late hour* fuch prurient ears as thefe ?

Is thy poor pride contented to receive   65

Such tranfitory fame as fools can give ?

Fools who unconfcious of the critic's laws,

Rain in fuch fhow'rs their indiftinct applaufe.

That THOU, even THOU, who liv'st upon renown,

And with eternal puffs infult'st the town,   70

Intrant, et tremulo fcalpuntur ubi intima verfu.

[h] Tun' vetule auriculis alienis colligis efcas ?

Auriculis quibus et dicas cute perditus ohe !

NOTES.

* I learn from Della Crufca's lamentations that he
is declined into the vale of years; that the women
fay to him, as they formerly faid to Anacreon, Γιρων ιι·
and that Love, about two years fince,

> " —— tore his name from his bright page,
> And gave it to approaching age."

Art forc'd at length to check the idiot roar,

And cry, " For heaven's fweet fake, no more, no
" more !"

" But why (thou fay'ft) why am I learn'd, why
" fraught

" With all the priest and all the fage have
taught,

" If the huge mafs, within my bofom pent,   75

" Muft ftruggle there, defpairing of a vent ?"

¹ Thou learn'd ! Alas, for Learning ! She is
fped.

And hast thou dimm'd thy eyes, and rack'd thy
head

And broke thy reft for THIS, for THIS alone ?

And is thy knowledge nothing if not known ? 80

Quo didiciffe, nifi hóc fermentum, et quæ femel
intus

Innata eft, rupto jecore exierit caprificus ?

En pallor, feniumque. ¹O mores ! ufque adeone

Scire tuum, nihil est, nifi te fcire hoc, fciat alter ?

C 2

O fool, fool, fool!—ᵏ But ſtill, thou crieſt, 'tis
    ſweet

To hear " That's HE !" from every one we
    meet ;

That's he whom critic Bell declares divine,

For whom the fair diurnal laurels twine ;

Whom Magazines, Reviews, conſpire to praiſe, 85

And Greathead calls the Homer of our days.

    F.   And is it nothing, then, to hear our name

Thus blazon'd by the GENERAL VOICE of
    fame ?

    P.   Nay, it were every thing, did THAT diſ-
    penſe

The ſober verdict found by taſte and ſenſe.   90

But mark OUR jury.   O'er the flowing bowl,

When wine has drown'd all energy of ſoul,

ᵏ At pulchrum eſt digito monſtrari, et dicier, Hic
    eſt :

Ten cirratorum centum dictata fuiſſe

Pro nihilo pendes ? Ecce inter pocula quærunt

Romulidæ ſaturi, quid dia poemata narrent.

Ere FARO comes (a dreary interval !)

For fome fond fafhionable lay they call.   R |

Here the fpruce enfign, tottering on his chair,   95

With lifping accent, and affected air,

Recounts the wayward fate* of that poor poet,

Who born for anguifh, and difpos'd to fhew it,

Hic aliquis, cui circum humeros hyacinthina
     læna eft,

Rancidulum quiddam balba de nare locutus,

NOTES.

* Recounts the wayward fate.—In the INTERVIEW
(fee the Britifh Album) the lover finding his miftrefs
inexorable, comforts himfelf, and juftifies her, by
boafting how well he can play the fool. And never
did Don Quixote exhibit half fo many extravagant
tricks in the Sierra Morena, for the *beaux yeux* of
his Dulcinea, as our diftracted amorofo threatens to
perform for the no lefs beautiful ones of Anna Matilda.

    " Yes, I will prove that I deferve my fate,
    Was born for anguifh, and was form'd for hate ;
    With fuch tranfcendent woe will breathe my
       figh,
    " That envying fiends fhall think it ecftafy," &c.

C 3

Did yet fo aukwardly his means employ,

That gaping fiends mistook his grief for joy. 100

   Lost in amaze at language fo divine,

The audience hiccup, and exclaim, " Damn'd

   fine !"

And are not now the author's afhes blest ?

Now lies the turf not lightly on his breaft ?

Do not fweet violets now around him bloom ? 105

Laurels now burst fpontaneous from his tomb.

   F. This is mere mockery : and (in your ear)

Reafon is ill refuted by a fneer.

Is praife an evil ? Is there to be found

One fo indifferent to its foothing found,   110

As not to wifh hereafter to be known,

And make a long futurity his own ;

Rather than—

     P.—With 'Squire Jerningham defcend

To pastry-cooks and moths, " and there an

   end !"

Phyllidas, Hypfipylas, vatum et plorabile fi quid

Eliquat, et tenero fupplantat verba palato.

¹ O thou that deign'st this homely fcene to
    fhare,   .   115
Thou know'st when chance *(tho' this indeed be*
    rare*)

Affenfere viri.   Nunc non cinis ille poetæ
Felix ? non levior cippus nunc imprimit offa ?
Laudant convivæ nunc non e manibus illis,
Nunc non e tumulo, fortunataque favilla.
¹ Quifquis es, O, modo quem ex adverfo dicere feci,
Non ego, cum fcribo, fi forte quid aptius exit,
Quando hoc rara avis eft, fi quid tamen aputius
    exit,
Laudari metuam ; neque enim mihi cornea fibra eft :
Sed recti finemque extremumque effe recufo

NOTES.

* To fee how a Crufcan can blunder! Mr. Par-
fons thus politely comments on this unfortunate he-
miftich.
  " Thou loweft of the imitating race,
  " Thou imp of fatire, and thou foul difgrace ;
  " Who calleft *each* coarfe phrafe a lucky hit, &c."

With random gleams of wit has grac'd my lays,

Thou know'ft too well how I have relifh'd praife.

Not mine the foul that pants not after fame—

Ambitious of a poet's envied name, 120

I haunt the facred fount, athirft to prove

The grateful influence of the ftream I love.

And yet, my friend (though ftill at praife beftow'd

Mine eye has gliften'd, and my cheek has
glow'd)

Nafcentur violæ ? Rides, ait, et nimis uncis

Naribus indulges : an erit, qui velle recufet

Os populi meruiffe ; et cedro digna locutus,

Linquere nec fcombros metuentia carmina, nec
thus ?

NOTES.

Alas! no: I call few of them fo. But this is of a piece with his qui-pro-quò on the preface to the Mæviad—where, on my faying I had laid the poem afide for two years, he exultingly exclaims, " Soh! it was two years in hand then!"

Mr. P. is highly celebrated, I am told, for his fkill in driving a bargain : it is to be prefumed he does it with his fpe£tacles on !

Yet when I prostitute the lyre to gain   125
The eulogies that wait each modiſh strain,
May the ſweet Muſe my groveling hopes with-
    stand,
And tear the strings indignant from my hand ;
Nor think that, while my verſe too much I prize,
Too much th' applauſe of faſhion I deſpiſe ; 130
For mark to what 'tis given, and then declare,
Mean tho' I am, if it be worth my care.
Is it not given to Este's unmeaning daſh,
To Topham's fustian, Colman's flippant traſh,
To Andrews'* doggrel—where three wits com-
    bine   135
To Morton's catch-word†, Greathead's ideot line,
And Holcroft's Shug-lane cant, and Merry's
    Moorfields whine ‡.

Euge tuum, & belle; nam belle hoc, excute
    totum.

NOTES.

* Andrews.—Such is the reputation this gentleman
has obtained for Epilogue writing, that the minor

^m Skill'd in one ufeful fcience at the leaft,

The great man comes, and fpreads a fumptuous

   feaft :

Quid non intus habet ? Non hic eft Ilias Atti

Ebria veratro ; non fi qua elegidia crudi

Dictarunt proceres ; non quidquid denique lectis

^m Scribitur in citreis : calidum fcis ponere fumen,

Scis comitem horridulum trita donare lacerna :

Et verum, iniquis, amo ; verum mihi dicite de me.

Qui pote ? vis dicam ? nugaris——

NOTES.

poets of the day, defpairing of emulating, are now only folicitous of affifting him—happy if they can obtain admiffion for a couplet or two into the body of his immortal works, and thus fecure to themfelves a fmall portion of that popular applaufe fo lavifhly, and fo juftly beftowed on every thing that bears the figna-ture of Miles Andrews! See " the PROLOGUE to the CURE FOR THE HEART ACH by Miles Andrews, and ASSISTANTS.

 † Morton's catch-word.—WONDERFUL is the profundity of the Bathos! I thought O'Keefe had reached the. bottom of it : but as uncle Bowling fays, I thought a d—n'd lie—for Holcroft, Reynolds, and

Then, when his guefts behold the prize at ftake, 140
And thirft and hunger only are awake,

Vos, O patricius fanguis, quos vivere fas eft
Occipiti cæco, pofticæ occurrite fannæ.

NOTES.

Morton, have funk infinitely beneath him. They
have happily found

> In the *loweft* deep a *lower* ftill,

and perfevere in exploring it with an emulation which
does them honour.

Will pofterity believe this facetious triumverate
could think nothing more to be neceffary to the
conftruction of a play, than an eternal repetition of
fome contemptible vulgarity, fuch as That's your fort
Hey, damme! What's to pay! Keep moving, &c.!
They will: for they will have blockheads of their
own; who will found their claims to celebrity on
fimilar follies. What, however, they will never cre‐
dit is—that thefe drivellings of ideotifm, thefe catch‐
words, fhould actually preferve their refpective au‐
thors from being hiffed off the ftage. No, they will
not believe that an Englifh audience could be fo be‐
fotted, fo brutified as to receive fuch fenfelefs excla‐

My friends, he cries, what do the galleries fay,

And what the boxes, of my laft new play ?

Speak freely, tell me all—come, be fincere ;

For truth, you know, is mufic to my ear.　145

They fpeak ? Alas, they cannot ! But fhall I ;

I who receive no bribe, who dare not lie ?

NOTES.

mations with burfts of laughter, with peals of applaufe. I cannot believe it myfelf; though I have
witneffed it. Haud credo—if I may reverfe the good
father's pofition—Haud credo, quia poffibile eft.

‡ Merry's Moorfields' whine.—In a moft wretched
rhapfody of incomprehenfible nonfenfe, addreffed by
this gentleman to Mrs. Robinfon, which fhe in her
valuable poems (page 100) calls a charming compofition, abounding in lines of exquifite beauty, is the
following rant :

> Conjure up demons from the main
> Storms upon ftorms indignant heap,
> Bid ocean howl, and nature weep,
> Till the Creator *blufh to fee*
> *How horrible his world can be :*
> While I will GLORY TO BLASPHEME,
> AND MAKE THE JOYS OF HELL MY THEME.

The reader, perhaps, wonders what dreadful event
gave birth to thefe fearful imprecations. As far as I

This then— " that worfe was never writ before,

Nor worfe will be—till thou fhalt write once
more. "

ⁿ Blest be " two-headed Janus !" tho' inclin'd, 150

No waggifh stork can peck at him behind ;

He no wry mouth, no lolling tongue can fear,

Nor the brifk twinkling of an afs's ear.

But you, ye St. Johns, curs'd with one poor head,

Alas ! what mockeries have not ye to dread ! 155

ⁿ O Jane, a tergo quem nulla ciconia pinfit,

Nec manus auriculas imitata eft mobilis albas,

Nec linguæ, quantum fitiat canis Apula, tantæ.

NOTES.

can colleft, it was—the aforefaid Mrs. Robinfon's
not opening her eyes ! ! ! Surely it is moft devoutly to
be wifhed that thefe poor creatures would recolleft,
amidft their frigid ravings, and common-place extra-
vagancies, that excellent maxim of Pope—

" Perfift, by nature, reafon, tafte, unaw'd ;

" But learn, ye Dunces, not to fcorn your God."

* Hear now our guests :—The critics, Sir! they
    cry—
Merit like yours the critics may defy.
But this indeed they fay—" Your varied rhymes,
At once the boast and envy of the times,
In every page, fong, fonnet, what you will,   160
Shew boundlefs genius, and unrivall'd fkill.

    If comedy be yours, the fearching strain
Gives a fweet pleafure, fo chastis'd by pain,
Than e'en the guilty at their fufferings fmile,
And blefs the lancet, tho' they bleed the while.165

---

* Quis populi fermo eft ? quis enim, nifi carmina
    molli
Nunc demum numero fluere, ut per leve feveros
Effundat junctura ungues——
Sive opus in mores, in luxum, in prandia regum,
Dicere res grandes nostro dat Mufa poetæ.
Ecce modo heroas fenfus afferre videmus
Nugari folitos Græcè, nec ponere lucum

If tragedy, th' impaffion'd numbers flow
In all the fad variety of woe,
With fuch a liquid lapfe, that they betray
The breast unwares, and steal the foul away."

Thus fool'd, the moon-struck tribe, whofe best
     effays   170
Sunk in acrostics and in roundelays,
To loftier labours now pretend a call,
And bustle in heroics, one and all.
E'en Bertie burns of gods and chiefs to fing—
Bertie who lately twitter'd to the string   175
His namby-pamby madrigals of love,
In the dark dingles of a glittering grove,
Where airy lays,* woven by the hand of morn,
Were hung to dry upon a cobweb thorn ! ! !

Artifices, nec rus faturum laudare.—Euge, poeta !

NOTES.

* Where airy lays, &c.
    " Was it the fhuttle of the morn
    " That hung upon the cobweb'd thorn

Happy the foil where bards like mufhrooms
    rife,   180
And afk no culture but what Byfhe fupplies !
Happier the bards who, write whate'er they will,
Find gentle readers to admire them ftill !

    Some love the verfe that like Maria's flows
No rubs to ftagger, and no fenfe to pofe ;   185
Which read, and read, you raife your eyes in
    doubt,
And gravely wonder what it is about.
Thefe fancy " BELL'S POETICS" only fweet,
And intercept his hawkers in the ftreet ;

Eft nunc Brifæi quem venofus liber Acci
Sunt quos Pacuviufque, et verrucofa moretur
Antiopa, ærumnis cor luctificabile fulta.

NOTES.

    " Thy airy lay ? Or did it rife,
    " In thoufand rich enamell'd dyes,
    " To greet the noon-day fun," &c.
                      BELL'S ALBUM, vol. ii.

There, fmoaking hot, inhale *.MIT YENDA's
  ftrains,   190
And the rank fume of TONY PASQUIN's brains.†

NOTES.

* MIT YENDA. This is Mr. Tim, alias Mr.
Timothy Adney, a moft pertinacious gentleman, who
makes a confpicuous figure in the papers under the
ingenious fignature above cited; being, as the reader
already fees, his own name read backward. " Gentle
dulnefs ever loves a joke!"

Of his prodigious labours I have nothing by me
but the following ftanza, taken from what he calls
his Poor Man :
 Reward the bounty of your generous hand,
  Your head each night in comfort fhall be *laid*,
 And plenty fmile throughout your fertile land,
  While I do haften to the filent *grave*.

" Good morrow, my worthy mafters and miftreffes
all; and a merry Chriftmas to you."

I find I have been guilty of a mifnomer. Mr. Adney having politely informed me, fince the above was
written, that his chriftian name is not Timothy but
Thomas. The Anagram in queftion, therefore muft
be MOT YENDA; omitting the H *euphoniæ gratia*;
I am happy in an opportunity of doing juftice to fo
correct a gentleman, and I pray him to continue his
valuable labour.

D

Others, like Kemble, on black letter pore,

And what they do not underſtand, adore ;

NOTES.

† TONY PASQUIN.—I have too much reſpeᴄt for my reader to affront him with any ſpecimens of this man's poetry, at once licentious and dull beyond example : at the ſame time I cannot reſiſt the temptation of preſenting him with the following ſtanzas, written by a friend of mine, and ſufficiently illuſtrative of the charaᴄter in queſtion :

TO ANTHONY PASQUIN, Eſq.

Why doſt thou tack, moſt ſimple Anthony,
    The name of *Paſquin* to thy ribbald ſtrains ?
Is it a fetch of wit, to let us ſee
    Thou, like that ſtatue, art devoid of brains ?

But thou miſtak'ſt : for know, tho' Paſquin's head
    Be full as hard, and near as thick, as thine ;
Yet has the world admiring on it read
    Many a keen gibe, and many a ſportive line.

While nothing from thy jobbernowl can ſpring
    But impudence and filth ; for out, alas !
Do what we will, 'tis ſtill the ſame vile thing,
    Within, all brick-duſt—and without, all braſs.

Buy at vaſt ſums the *traſh* of ancient days,

And draw on prodigality for praiſe.　　190

Theſe, when ſome lucky hit, or lucky price,

Has bleſs'd them with " *The Boke of good ad-*

vice,"

Hos pueris monitus patres infundere lippos

Cum videas, quærifque unde hæc ſartago lo-

quendi

NOTES.

Then blot the name of Pasquin from thy page :
Thou feeft it will not thy poor riff-raff fell.
Some other wouldft thou take ? I dare engage
John Williams, or Tom Fool, will do as
well.

Tony has taken my friend's advice, and now fells
or attempts to fell " his riff-raff " under the name of
John Williams.

It has been reprefented to me, that I fhould do
well to avoid all mention of this man ; from a
confideration that one fo loft to every fenfe of decen-
cy and fhame, was a fitter objeét for the Beadle

D 2

For *ekes* and *algates* only deign to feek,

And live upon a *whilome* for a week *.

 And can we when fuch mope-eyed dolts are
 plac'd   200
By thoughtlefs fafhion on the throne of tafte—

Venerit in linguas ? unde istud dedecus ?——

` Fur es, ait Pedio.   Pedius quid ? crimina rafis

NOTES.

than the Mufe.   This has induced me to lay afide
a fecond caftigation which I had prepared for
him, though I do not think it expedient to omit
what I had formerly written.

 HERE on the rack of Satire let him lie,
 Fit garbage for the hell-hound Infamy.

 One word more.   I am told there are men fo
weak as to deprecate this miferable object's abufe,
and fo vain, fo defpicably vain, as to tolerate his.
praife—for fuch I have nothing but pity ;—though
the fate of Haftings, fee the " Pin-bafket to the Children of Thefpis," holds out a dreadful leffon to the
latter—but fhould there be a man, or a woman—
however high their rank—bafe enough to purchafe
the venal pen of this mifcreant for the fake of tra-

Say, can we wonder whence this jargon flows,

This motley fuftian, neither verfe nor profe,

This old new language that defiles our page,

The refufe and the fcum of every age?   205

Librat in antithetis ; doctas pofuiffe figuras

Laudatur ; bellum hoc. Hoc bellum ? An Ro-

  mule ceves ?

NOTES.

ducing innocence and virtue; then——I was about
to — —; but 'tis not neceffary: the profligate
cowards who employ Antony can know no feverer
punifhment than the fupport of a man whofe acquaintance is infamy, and whofe touch is poifon.

* Others like Kemble, &c.—Tho' no great Cata-
logue hunter, I love to look into fuch marked ones as
fall in my way. That of poor Dood's books amufed
me not a little. It exhibited many inftances of BLACK
LETTER mania ; and, what is more to my purpofe,
a transfer of much " trafh of ancient days," to the
fortunate Mr. Kemble. For example.

           £. s d

Firft part of the tragicall Raigne of Seli-
  mus Emperour of the Turks - - - 1 11 6

D 3

Lo, Beaufoy * tells of Afric's barren fand
In all the flow'ry phrafe of fairy land :

$£. \quad s. \quad d.$

Jacob and Efau, a Mery and Whittie
 Comedie - - - - -   3   5   0
Look About You, a comedie - - - - - .5   7   6
The tragedie of T. Nero, Rome's Greateft
 Tyraunte, &c. &c. - - - - - - - 1   4   0
How are we ruined !

* Lo ! Beaufoy, &c.—" The feet are *accommodated*
with fhoes, †, and the head is *protected* by a—woollen
nightcap."
     AFRICAN ASSOCIATION, p. 139.

---

† Shoes.—By your leave, mafter critic, here is a fmall
overfight in your quotation. The gentleman does not fay
their feet are accommodated with *fhoes*, but with *flippers*.
For the reft, *accomodate*, as I learn, is a fcholar-like word,
and a word of exceeding great propriety. *Accommodate!* it
comes from *accommodo :* that is, when a man's feet are, as
they fay, accommodated ; or when they are—being—whereby
they may be thought to be accommodated : which is an
excellent thing.
     PRINTER's DEVIL.

There Fezzan's thrum-capp'd tribes, Turks,
 Chriftians, Jews,
Accommodate, ye gods ! their feet with fhoes.
There *meagre* fhrubs *inveterate* mountains
 grace,   210
And *brufhwood* breaks the *amplitude of fpace.*
Perplex'd with terms fo vague and undefin'd,
I blunder on ; till wilder'd, giddy, blind,
Where'er I turn, on clouds I feem to tread ;
And call for Mandeville to eafe my head.   215

 Oh for the good old times ! When all was new,
And every hour brought prodigies to view,
Our fires in unaffected language told
Of ftreams of amber, and of rocks of gold :

 " From this fcene of gladfome contraft, i. e. from
the mountain of Zillau (p. 288), whofe rugged fides
are marked with fcanty fpots of brufhwood, and en-
riched with ftores of water, to the long afcent of the
broad rock of Gerdobah (p. 289), from whofe inflexi-
ble barrennefs little is to be got—from this fcene, I
fay, of gladfome contraft to the *inveterate* mountains
of Gegogib, &c."

Full of their theme, they fpurn'd all idle art, 220
And the plain tale was trufted to the heart.
Now all is changed! We fume and fret, poor
     elves ;
Lefs to difplay our fubject, than ourfelves :
Whate'er we paint—a grot, a flow'r, a bird,
Heavens, how we fweat, laborioufly abfurd ! 225
Words of gigantic bulk, and uncouth found,
In rattling triads the long fentence bound ;
While points with points, with periods periods
     jar,
And the whole work feems one continued war !
Is not THIS fad ?

       F. " 'TIS pitiful, God knows,   230
" 'TIS wondrous pitiful." E'en take the profe ;
But for the poetry—oh, that my friend,
I ftill afpire—nay, fmile not—to defend.

NOTES.

" In the long courfe of a feven-days paffage, the
traveller is fcarcely fenfible that a few fpots of thin
and *meagre* brufhwood flightly interrupt the vaft
expanfe of flerility, and diminifh the amplitude of
defolation ! ! !"

ᴾ You praife our fires, but, though they wrote
    with force,
Their rhymes were vicious, and their diction
    coarfe ;   235
We want their *ftrength* : agreed.   But we atone
For that, and more, by *fweetnefs* all our own.
For instance—"* Hasten to the lawny vale,
" Where yellow morning breathes her faffron
    gale,
" And bathes the landfcape—"

                    P. Pfhaw ! I have it here : 240
" A voice feraphic grafps my listening ear :
" Wond'ring I gaze ; when lo ! methought afar,
" More bright than dauntlefs day's imperial star,
" A godlike form advances."

ᴾ Sed numeris decor eft, et junctura addita
    crudis.

NOTES.

* Haften, &c.—This and the following quotation
are taken from the " Laurel of Liberty," a work on
which the great author moft juftly refts his claims to
immortality.

F. You fuppofe

Thefe lines perhaps too turgid ; what of
thofe ?   245
" THE MIGHTY MOTHER ¶—"

                    P. Now 'tis plain you fneer,
For * Weston's felf could find no femblance
    here.
Weston ! who flunk from truth's imperious light,
Swells like a filthy toad, with fecret fpite,

───────────────────────

Ut ramale vetus prægrandi fubere coctum.
Claudere fic verfum didicit Berecynthius Atys,
Et qui cæruleum dirimebat Nerea Delphin.
Sic coftam longo fubduximus Appennino.
" ¶ Arma virum" nonne hoc fpumofum et cortice
    pingui ?

                    NOTES.

    * Wefton.—This indefatigable gentleman has been
attacking the moral character of Pope in the Gentleman's Magazine, with all the virulence of Gildon,
all the impudence of Smedley, and all the ignorance
of Curl and his affociates.

And, envying the fair fame he cannot hope, 250

Spits his black venom at the dust of Pope.

Reptile accurs'd!—O memorable long,

If there be force in virtue or in song,

O injur'd bard! accept the grateful strain,

That I, the humblest of the tuneful train, 255

With glowing heart, yet trembling hand repay

For many a penfive, many a fprightly lay:

So may thy varied verfe, from age to age,

Inform the fimple, and delight the fage!

NOTES.

What the views of the immaculate Sylvanus may
be, in ftanding cap in hand, and complacently holding
open the door of the temple, for near two years, to
this * " execrable" Eroftratus, I know not. He cannot fure be weak enough to fuppofe an obfcure fcribbler like this has any charges to bring againft our great
poet, that efcaped the vigilant malevolence of the
Weftons of the Dunciad. Or if ever, from the na-
tural goodnefs of his heart, he cherifhed fo laudable
a fuppofition, he ought (whatever it may coft him)
to forego it: when, after twenty months, nothing is
produced but an exploded accufation taken from the

* Such is the epithet applied to Pope by the virtuous indignation of this amiable traducer of worth and genius!

While canker'd Wefton, and his loathfome
      rhymes, 260

Stink in the nofe of all fucceeding times !

    Enough[r]. But where (for thefe, you feem to fay,

Are famples of the high, heroic lay) 260

Where are the foft, the tender ftrains, that call

For the moift eye, bow'd head, and lengthen'd
      drawl ? 266

---

[r] Quidnam igitur tenerum & laxa cervice legen-
dum ?

NOTES.

moft common edition of the Dunciad ; which, as nothing but Weftonian rancour could firft make, fo
nothing but Weftonian ftupidity can now revive.

    It has been fuggefted to me, that this nightman
of literature defigns to reprint as much as can be collected of the heroes of the Dunciad.—If it be fo, the
dirty work of traducing Pope may be previoufly neceffary ; and prejudice itfelf muft own, that he has
fhewn uncommon penetration in the felection of the
blind and outrageous mercenary now fo laborioufly
employed in it.

    Whatever be the defign, the proceedings are by no
means inconfiftent with the plan of a work which

Lo! here——" *Canſt thou, Matilda, urge my
    fate,

" And bid me mourn thee?—yes, and mourn too
    late!

" O raſh, ſevere decree! my maddening brain
" Cannot the ponderous agony ſuſtain ;

Torva Mimalloneis implerunt cornua bombis,
Et raptum vitulo caput ablatura ſuperbo
Baſſaris——

NOTES.

may not unaptly be ſtyled THE CHARNEL-HOUSE OF
REPUTATION, and which from the days of Lauder
to the preſent, has delighted to aſperſe every thing
venerable amongſt us—which accuſed Swift of luſt,
and Addiſon of drunkenneſs; which inſulted the
aſhes of Toup while they were yet warm, and gib-
beted poor Henderſon alive; which affected to ido-
lize the great and good Howard, while idolatry was
painful to him; and the moment he fell, glorioufly
fell, in the exerciſe of the moſt ſublime virtue, at-
tempted to ſtigmatiſe him as a brute and a monſter!

    * Canſt thou Matilda, &c. (vide Album, vol. ii.)—
Matilda! " nay then, I'll never truſt a madman
again." It was but a few minutes ſince, that Mr.
Merry died for the love of Laura Maria; and now is

" But forth I rufh, from vale to mountain
    run,   270
" And with my mind's thick gloom obfcure the
    fun."

   ' Heavens! if our ancient vigour were not fled,
Could VERSE like this be written or be read ?
VERSE ! THAT's the mellow fruit of toil intenfe,
Infpir'd by genius, and inform'd by fenfe ; 275
THIS, the abortive progeny of Pride
And Dulnefs, gentle pair, for aye allied ;
Begotten without thought, born without pains,
The ropy drivel of rheumatic brains.

 ' Hæc fierent, fi testiculi vena ulla paterni
Viveret in nobis ? fumma delumbe faliva,
Hoc natat in labris : et in udo est Mænas et Atys ;
Nec pluteum cædit, nec demorfos fapit ungues.

he going to do the fame thing for the love of Anna
Matilda ?
   What the ladies may fay to fuch a fwain, I know not ;
but certainly he is too prone to run wild, die, &c. &c.
Such indeed is the combuftible nature of this gentleman,

F. 'So let it be: and yet, methinks, my
      friend,   280

Silence were wife, where fatire will not mend.
Why wound the feelings of our noble youth,
And grate their tender ears with odious truth?
They cherifh *Arno, and his flux of fong,
And hate the man who tells 'em they are
      wrong.   280

---

‡ Sed quid opus teneras mordaci radere vero
Auriculas? vide fis, ne majorum tibi forte

NOTES.

that he takes fire at every female fignature in the papers: and I remember, that when Olaudo Equiano,
(who, for a black, is not ill-featured) tried his hand at
a foft fonnet, and by miftake fubfcribed it *Olauda*, Mr,
Merry fell fo defperately in love with him, and "yelled
"out fuch fyllables of dolour" in confequence of it,
that "the pitiful hearted" negro was frightened at the
mifchief he had done, and tranfmitted in all hafte the
following correction to the editor——" For *OlaudA*,
" pleafe to read *OlaudO*, the black MAN."

   * Of this *fpes altera Romæ*, this fecond hope of
the age, the following ftanzas will afford a fufficient
fpecimen. They are taken from a ballad which

Thy fate already I forefee.   My Lord
With cold refpect will freeze thee from his board ;
And his Grace cry, " Hence with your fapient
    fneer !
" Hence! we defire no currifh critic here."

Limina frigefcant : fonat hic de nare canina

NOTES.

Mr. Bell, an admirable judge of thefe matters,
calls a " very mellifluous one ; eafy, artlefs, and
unaffected."

   Gently o'er the rifing *billows*
    Softly fteals the bird of night,
   Ruftling thro' the *bending willows* ;
    Fluttering pinions *mark* her flight.

   Whither now in *filence bending,*
    Ruthlefs winds *deny thee reft* ;
   Chilling *night-dews* faft defcending
    Gliften on thy downy breaft.

   Seeking fome kind hand to guide thee,
    Wiftful turns thy *fearful* eye ;
   Trembling as the willows *hide* thee,
    Shelter'd from th' inclement fky.

  The ftory of this poor owl, who was at one and
the fame time at fea and on land, filent and noify,

P. Enough. ᶠ Thank heaven! my error now
  I fee,
And all fhall be divine henceforth for me : ·

Litera. ᶠ Per me equidem fint omnia protinus alba,

NOTES.

fheltered and expofed, is continued through a few
more of thefe " mellifluous" ftanzas : which the
reader, I doubt not, will readily forgive me for
omitting ; more efpecially if he reads the ORACLE,
a PAPER honoured—as the grateful editor very
properly has it—by the effufions of this " artlefs"
gentleman above all others.

N. B. On looking again, I find the OWL to be a
Nightingale.—N'importe.

It was faid of Theophilus Cibber (I think by
Goldfmith), that as he grew older, he grew never the
better. Much the fame (mutatis mutandis) may be
faid of the gentlemen of the Baviad. After an interval of two years, I find the " mellifluous" ARNO
celebrating Mrs. Robinfon's Novel in ftrains like
thefe :

E

Yes, Andrew's doggrell, Greathead's idiot line,
And Morton's catch-word, all, forfooth, di-
  vine!   290
  F. 'Tis well. Here let th' indignant stricture
  ceafe,
And LEEDS at length enjoy his fool in peace.

———————————————

Nil moror: euge, omnes, omnes bene miræ
  eritis res.
Hoc juvat : hic iniquis, veto quifquam faxit
  oletum.

NOTES.

For the ORACLE.

SONNET to Mrs. ROBINSON,

Upon reading her VANCENZA.

WHAT never-ceafing Mufic! From the throne
 Where fweeteft SENSIBILITY enfhrin'd
Pours out her tender triumphs, all alone
 To every murmuring breeze of paffing wind!

P. Come then, around their works a circle
    draw,
And near it plant the dragons of the law;
With labels writ, " Critics far hence remove, 295
" Nor dare to cenfure what the great approve."
I go. ᵍ Yet Hall could lafh with noble rage
The purblind patron of a former age,

Pinge duos angues: pueri, facer est locus, extra
Mejite; ᵍ difcedo: fecuit Lucilius urbem,

NOTES.

O, bleft with all the lovely lapfe of Song,
    That bathes with pureft balm the foften'd breaft,
I fee thee urge thy Fancy's courfe along
    The folemn glooms of GOTHIC piles *unbleft*.

VANCENZA rifes—o'er her time-touch'd fpires
    GUILT *unreveal'd* hovers with killing dew,
Fruftrates the fondnefs of the VIRGIN's fires,
    And bares the *murd'rous* CASKET to her view.

The thrilling pulfe creeps back upon each Heart,
And HORROR lords it by thy facinating Art.

                     ARNO.

Et vitula TU dignus, et HÆC! The Novel is worthy of the Poetry; the Poetry of the Novel.

And laugh to fcorn th' eternal fonnetteer
Who made goofe-pinions and white rags fo dear.
Yet Oldham in his rude, unpolifh'd strain, 301
Could hifs the clamorous, and deride the vain,
Who bawl'd their rhymes inceffant thro' the .
  town,
Or brib'd the hawkers for a day's renown.
Whate'er the theme, with honest warmth they
  wrote,   305
Nor car'd what Mutius of their freedom thought :
Yet profe was venial in that happy time,
And life had other bufinefs than to rhyme.
 h And may not I—now this pernicious peft,
This metromania, creeps thro' every breast ; 310
Now fools and children void their brains by loads,
And itching grandams fpawl lafcivious odes ;

———————————————————

Te Lupe, te Muti, & genuinum fregit in illis.
h Men' mutire nefas, nec clam, nec cum fcrobe ?
  Nufquam.
Hic tamen infodiam. Vidi, vidi ipfe, libelle :

Now lords and dukes, curs'd with a fickly taste,

While Burns' pure healthful nurture runs to
    waste,

Lick up the fpittle of the bed rid mufe,   315

And riot on the fweepings of the stews ;

Say, may not I expofe—

        F. No—'tis unfafe.

Prudence my friend.

      P. What ! not deride, not laugh ?

Well ! thought at least is free—

        F. O yet forbear.

P. Nay, then, I'll dig a pit, and bury there

The dreadful truth that fo alarms thy fears : 320

THE TOWN, THE TOWN, GOOD PIT, HAS
    ASSES EARS !

Thou think'st perhaps, this wayward fancy
    strange ;

So think thou still ; yet would not I exchange

Auriulas afini Mida rex habet. Hoc ego oper-
    tum,

Hoc ridere meum tam nil, nulla tibi vendo

E 3

The secret humour of this simple hit   325
For all the Albums that were ever writ.
Of this no more. O THOU (if yet there be
One bosom from this vile infection free),
THOU who canst thrill with joy, or glow with
       ire,
As the great masters of the song inspire   330
Canst hang enamour'd o'er the magic page,
Where desperate ladies desperate lords engage,
Gnomes, Sylphs, and Gods the fierce contention
       share,
And heaven and earth hang trembling on a hair ;
Canst quake with horror while Emilia's charms
Against a brother point a brother's arms,   335
And trace the fortune of the varying fray,
While hour on hour flits unperceived away—

***

Iliade.   Audaci quicunque afflate Cratino,
Iratum Eupolidem prægrandi cum sene palles,
Aspice & hæc, si forte aliquid decoctius audis.

Approach : 'twixt hope and fear I wait. O deign
To caſt a glance on this incondite ſtrain :   340
Here, if thou find one thought but well expreſt,
One ſentence higher finiſh'd than the reſt,
Such as may win thee to proceed awhile,
And ſmooth thy forehead with a gracious ſmile,
I aſk no more. ¹ But far from me the throng, 345
Who fancy fire in Laura's vapid ſong,
Who Anna's bedlam-rant for ſenſe can take,
And over * Edwin's mewlings keep awake ;

Inde vaporata lector mihi ferveat aure,
¹ Non hic, qui in crepidas Graiorum ludere geſtit,
Sefe aliquem credens, Italo quod honore ſupinus

NOTES.

* *Edwin's Mewlings*, &c.)—We come now to a
character of high reſpect, the profound Mr. T.
Vaughan, who, under the alluring ſignature of Edwin, favours us from time to time with a melancholy
poem on the death of a bug, the flight of an earwig,
the miſcarriage of a cock-chaffer, or ſome other
event of equal importance.

Yes, far from me, whate'er their birth or place,

Thefe long-ear'd judges of the Phrygian race, 350

Fregerit heminas—

His laſt work was an Επιταφιον (bleſſings on his learning!), which I take for granted means *an Epitaph*, on a mouſe that broke her heart : and, as it was a matter of great conſequence, he very properly made the introduction as long as the poem itſelf. Hear how gravely he prologiſeth :

On a tame mouſe, which belonged to a lady who ſaved its life, conſtantly fed it, and even wept, poor lady! at its approaching death. The mouſe's eyes actually dropped out of its head, poor mouſe! THE DAY BE-FORE IT DIED.

Επιταφιον.

This feeling mouſe whoſe heart was warm'd
    By Pity's pureſt ray,
Becauſe her Miſtreſs dropt a tear,
    Wept both her eyes away.

By ſympathy depriv'd of light,
    She one day's darkneſs tried ;

Their cenfure and their praife alike I fcorn,
And hate the laurel by their followers worn!

The grateful tear no more could flow,
So lik'd it not, and died.

May we when others weep for us,
The debt with int'reft pay—
And, when the gen'rous fonts are dry,
Revert to native clay.

EDWIN.

Mr. T. Vaughan has afferted that he is not the
author of this matchlefs Επιταφιον, with fuch fpirit,
and retorted upon one Baviad (whom without all con-
troverfy the learned gentleman takes to be a man)
with fuch ftrength of argument, and elegance of
diction, that I fhould wrong both him and the reader,
to give it in any words but his own.

" Well faid, Baviad the correct!—And fo the
PROFOUND Mr. T. Vaughan, as you politely ftyle
him, writes under the alluring fignature of Edwin,
does he? and therefore a very proper fubject for your
fatiric malignity!—But fuppofe for a moment, as the
truth and the *fact* is, that this gentleman never did
ufe that fignature upon any occafion, in whatever he
may have written: Do not you the identical Baviad,

Let fuch, a tafk congenial to their powers,

At fales and auctions waste the morning hours,

His mane edictum, poft prandia Calliroën do.

NOTES.

in that cafe, for your unprovoked abufe of him, immediately fall under your own character of that
Nightman of Literature you fo liberally affign Wefton ? And like him too, if there is any truth in what
you fay or write, do you not

Swell like a filthy toad with fecret fpite ?

The ayes have it. And fhould you not be as well
verfed in your favourite Author's Fourth Satire, as
you are in the Firft, with your leave, I will *quote* from
it *two* emphatic lines :

" Into themfelves how few, how few defcend,
" And act, at home, the free impartial friend !
" None fee their own, but all with ready eye
" The pendent wallet on a neighbour fpy;
" And like a Baviad will recount his fhame,
" Tacking his *very errors* to *bis name.*"

ORACLE, 12th Jan.

Wile the dull noon away in Christie's fane, 355
And fnore the evening out at Drury lane ;
Lull'd by the twang of Benfley's nafal note,
And the hoarfe croak of Kemble's foggy throat.

NOTES.

And, to *whofe* name fhould they be tacked, but the
author's ? Let not the reader, however, imagine the
abfurdity to proceed from Perfius, or his ingenious
tranflator. " The truth and the faft is," that our
learned brother, having a fmall change to make in
the two laft lines, blundered them with his ufual
acutenefs into nonfenfe. He is not much more happy
when he calls WESTON " the Nightman of Literature." But when a gentleman does not know what
he writes, it is a little hard upon him to expeft he
fhould know what he reads.—After all Edwin or
not, our egregious friend is ftill the PROFOUND Mr.
T. Vaughan.

MÆVIAD.

Qui BAVIUM non odit, amet tua carmina MÆVI.

———————

IN the INTRODUCTION to the preceding pages, I have given a brief account of the rife and progrefs of that fpurious fpecies of poetry, which lately infefted this metropolis, and gave occafion to the BAVIAD.

I was not ignorant of what I expofed myfelf to, by the publication of that work. If abufe could have affected me, I fhould not probably have made a fet of people my enemies, habituated to ill language, and poffeffed of fuch convenient vehicles * for its diffemination. But

* Moft of thefe fafhionable writers were connected with the public prints. Della Crufca was a worthy

I never regarded it from such hands; and,
indeed, deprecated nothing but their praife. I
refpeft, in common with every man of fenfe,
the cenfure of the wife and good: but the
angry ebullitions of folly unmafked, and vanity
mortified, pafs by me, " like the idle wind ;"
or, if noticed, ferve merely to grace fome fucceeding edition of the Baviad.

I confefs, however, that the work was received
more favourably than I expefted. Bell, indeed,
and a few others, whofe craft I had touched,
vented their indignation in profe, and verfe : but,
on the whole, the clamour againft me was not
loud ; and was loft by infenfible degrees in the
applaufes of fuch as I was truly ambitious to
pleafe.

coadjutor of the mad and malignant idiot who con-
dufted the World. Arno, and Lorenzo, were either
proprietors or editors of another paper. Edwin and
Anna Matilda, were favoured contributors to feveral,
and Laura Maria from the fums fhe fquandered on
puffs, could command a corner in all.

Thus supported, the good effects of the satire (gloriosè loquor) were not long in manifesting themselves. Della Crusca appeared no more in the Oracle, and, if any of his followers ventured to treat the town with a soft sonnet, it was not, as before, introduced by a pompous preface. Pope and Milton resumed their superiority ; and Este and his coadjutors, silently acquiesced in the growing opinion of their incompetency, and shewed some sense of shame.

With this I was satisfied. I had taken up my pen for no other end : and was quietly retiring, with the idea that I had " done the state some service ;" and purposing to abandon for ever the cæstus, which a respectable critic fancies I wielded " with too much severity" ; when I was once more called into the lists*, by the re-appearance of some of the scattered enemy.

NOTES.

* I hope no one will do me the injustice to suppose that I imagine myself another Hercules, contending with Hydras, &c. Far from it. My enemies

F

It was not enough that the ftream of folly flowed more fparingly in the Oracle than before ; I was determined

To have the current in *that place* damm'd up ;

And accordingly began the prefent poem—for which, indeed, I had by this time other reafons. I had been told that there were ftill a few admirers of the Crufcan fchool, who thought the contempt I fhewed for it not fufficiently juftified by the few paffages I had produced. To filence thefe

---

NOTES.

cannot well have an humbler opinion of me, than I have of myfelf; and yet " if I am not afhamed of them, I am a foufed gurnet." Mere pecora inertia! The conteft is without danger, and the victory without glory. At the fame time I declare againft any undue advantage being taken of thefe conceffions. Though I knew the impotence of thefe literary Afkaparts, the town did not : and many a man, who now affects to pity me for wafting my ftrength upon unrefifting imbecility, would, not long fince, have heard their poems with applaufe, and their praifes with delight.

objections therefore, I thought it beſt to exhibit the tribe of Bell once more; and, as they paſſed in review before me, to make ſuch additional extracts* from their works, as ſhould put their demerits beyond the power of future queſtion.

I remembered that this gentleman in his excellent remarks on the Baviad, had charged the author with "befpattering *nearly* all the poetical eminence of the day." Anxious, therefore, to do impartial juſtice, I ran for the ALBUM, to diſcover whom I had ſpared. Here I read, " In this collection are names whom Genius will ever look upon as its *beſt* ſupporters ! Sheridan"—— what is " SAUL alſo among the Prophets !— Sheridan, Merry, Parſons, Cowley, Andrews, Jerningham, Colman, Topham, Robinſon, &c."

NOTES.

* I know it will ſaid that I have done it, uſque ad nauſeam. I confeſs it; and for the reaſon given above. And yet I can honeſtly aſſure the reader, that moſt, if not all, of the traſh I have quoted, paſſed with the authors for ſuperlative beauties; every ſecond word being printed either in italics, or capitals.

F 2

Thus furnished with " all" the poetical eminence of the day, I proceeded, as Mr. Bell says, to befpatter it; taking for the vehicle of my defign, a Satire of Horace—to which I was led by its fupplying me (amidft many happy allufions) with an opportunity, I was not unwilling to feize, of briefly noticing the prefent wretched ftate of dramatic poetry*.

NOTES.

* I know not if the ftage has been fo low, fince the days of Gammar Gurton, as at this hour. It feems as if all the blockheads in the kingdom had ftarted up, and exclaimed, *una voce*, Come ! let us write for the theatres. In this there is nothing, perhaps altogether new ; the ftriking and peculiar novelty of the times feems to be, that ALL * they write is received. Of the three parties concerned in this bufinefs, the writers and the managers feem the leaft cul-

---

* I recolleft but two exceptions. Merry's idiotical Opera, and Mrs. Robinfon's more idiotical Farce. To have failed where O'Keefe fucceeded, argues a degree of ftupidity fcarcely credible. Surely " ignorance itfelf is a planet" over the heroes and heroines of the Baviad !

When the Mæviad (fo I call the prefent poem) was nearly brought to a conclufion, I laid it afide. The times feemed unfavourable to fuch productions. Events of real importance were momentarily claiming the attention of the public; and the ftill voice of the mufes was not likely to be liftened to amidft the din of arms. After an

---

pable. If the town will have hufks, extraordinary pains need not be taken to find them any thing more palatable. But what fhall we fay of the town itfelf! The lower orders of the people are fo brutified by the lamentable follies of O'Keefe, and Cobbe, and Pillon, and I know not who—Sardi venales, each worfe than the other—that they have loft all relifh for fimplicity and genuine humour: nay, ignorance itfelf, unlefs it be grofs and glaring, cannot hope for " their moft fweet voices." And the higher ranks are fo mawkifhly mild, that they take with a placid fimper whatever comes before them : or, if they now and then experience a flight fit of difguft, have not refolution enough to exprefs it, but fit yawning and gaping in each others faces for a little encouragement in their pitiful forbearance.

F 3

interval of two years, however, circumftances, which it is not material to mention, have induced me to finifh, and truft it, without more preface, to the candour to which I am already fo highly indebted for the warm reception of the Baviad.

I fhould here conclude this introduction, already too long ; were it not for the fake of noticing the ftrange inconfiftency of the town. I hear that I am now breaking butterflies upon wheels! There was a time (it was when the Baviad firft appeared) that thefe butterflies were Eagles, and their obfcure and defultory flights, the objeƈt of univerfal envy and admiration. They are yet fo with too many : and furely no one can wifh another to continue under the infatuation from which himfelf is happily free, for want of a little additional exertion !

THE

MÆVIAD.

———

YES, I did say that Crufca's * " true fublime"
Lacked tafte, and fenfe, and every thing but
    rhyme ;

IMITATIONS.

Horace, Sat. 10. Lib. 1.

V. 1. Nempe incompofito dixi pede currere
    verfus

NOTES.

* Crufca's " true fublime." The words between
inverted commas in this, and the following verfes,

F 4

That Arno's " eafy ftrains" were coarfe and
    rough,
And Edwin's " matchlefs numbers" woeful ftuff.

IMITATIONS.

Lucill. Quis tam Lucili fautor inepte eft,
Ut non hoc fateatur ?

are Mr. Bell's. They contain, as the reader fees,
a fhort charaƈter of the works to which they are
refpeƈtively affixed. Though I have the misfortune
to differ from this gentleman in the prefent inftances,
yet I obferve fuch acutenefs of perception in his general criticifm, that I fhould have ftiled him the
" profound" inftead of the " gentle " Bell; if I
had not previoufly applied the epithet to a ftill
greater man, (abfit invidia diƈto) to—Mr. T.
Vaughan.

    I truft this incidental preference will create no jea-
loufy—for though, as Virgil properly remarks, " An
oaken ftaff EACH merits ;" yet I need not inform a
gentleman, who, like Mr. Bell, reads Shakefpeare
every day after dinner, that " if two men ride upon
a horfe, one of them muft ride behind."

And who—forgive, O gentle Bell! the word, 5
For it muſt out—who, prithee, ſo abſurd,
So muliſhly abſurd, as not to join
In this with me; ſave always THEE, and
    THINE!

Yet ſtill, the SOUL of candour! I allow'd
Their jingling elegies amuſed the croud;   10
That lords and dukes hung blubbering o'er each
    line,
That lady-critics wept, and cried " divine!"
That love-lorn prieſts reclined the penſive head,
And ſentimental enſigns, as they read,
Wiped the ſad drops of pity from their eye, 15
And burſt between a hiccup and a ſigh.

IMITATIONS.

V. 10, &c. ——— At idem quod ſale multo
Urbem defricuit, charta laudatur eadem.
Nec tamen hoc tribuens dederim quoque cætera :
    nam ſic
Et Laberî minos, ut pulchra poemata mirer.

Yet, not content, like horſe-leeches they come,

And ſplit my head with one eternal hum

For " more! more! more!" Away! For
          ſhould I grant

The full, the unreſerved applauſe, ye want, 20

St. John * might then my partial voice accuſe,

And claim my ſuffrage for his tragic muſe ;

IMITATIONS.

V. 17. The horſe-leech has two daughters,
crying, " Give! give!"

PROVERBS.

NOTES.

* St. John, &c. Having already obſerved in the
Introduction that the Mæviad was nearly finiſhed two
years ſince, and conſequently before the death of this
gentleman; I have only to add here, that though I
ſhould not have introduced into it any of the heroes
of the Baviad, quorum Flaminia tegitur cinis, atque
Latina, yet I ſcarce think it neceſſary to make any
changes for the ſake of omitting ſuch as have paſſed
ad plures, in the interval between writing and pub-
liſhing.

And Greathead *, rifing from his fhort difgrace,
Fling the forgotten " Regent" in my face ;
Bid me my cenfure, as I may, deplore,
And like my brother critics cry " Encore!"

NOTES.

The reader will find (v. 235) another inftance of my fmall pretenfions to prophecy; and probably regret it more than the prefent.

* Greathead's Regent. Of this tragedy, which was recommended to the world in more than one refpectable publication, as " the work of a SCHOLAR," I want words to exprefs my opinion. The plot of it was childifh, the conduct abfurd, the language unintelligible, the thoughts falfe and confufed, the metaphors incongruous, the general ftyle groveling and bafe, and, to fum up all in a word, the whole piece the moft execrable abortion of ftupidity that ever difgraced the ftage.

It is to be wifhed that Reviewers, fenfible of the influence their opinions neceffarily have on the public tafte, could diveft themfelves of their partialities, when they fit down to the execution of, what I hope they confider as, their folemn duty. We fhould not then find them, as in the inftance before us, recommending a work to favour, deferving univerfal reprobation and contempt.

Alas, my learned friends! for learn'd ye are,

...

IMITATIONS.

V. 27.. Ergo non fatis eft rifu diducere rictum
Auditoris; & eft quædam tamen hic quoque
virtus.

NOTES.

This is perhaps requiring too much; as it fup-
pofes them not poffeffed of the feelings of other
men. And yet—on confidering the importance of
the office they have affumed, and the good or evil
they have the means of difpenfing—I have on more
than one occafion lamented that they were

" No more but even mortals, and commanded
By fuch poor paffions as the maid that milks,
And does the meaneft chares."

It is but fair to obferve, however, that Mr. Parfons has added his all-fufficient fuffrage to that of
the Reviewers, in favour of Mr. Greathead's
abilities.

" O bard! to whom belongs
Each pureft fount of poefy!

As Bell will fay, or, if ye afk it, fwear ;

NOTES.

Who old Ilyffus' hallowed dews
In his own Avon dares infufe.
O favoured clime ! O happy age !
That boafts to fave a finking ftage"
A Greathead ! ! !

Gent. Mag.

When I read thefe, and other high founding praifes,
fcattered over Reviews, Magazines, Newfpapers, and
I know not what, without having feen any thing but
the Regent ; I was naturally led to fufpeft that Mr.
G. had fucceeded better in his fmaller pieces, and
thus juftified in fome degree the cry of his " learning, &c." But no. All was a blank !

Here follow a few famples of the " Ilyffean dews
infufed by Mr. Greathead into his own Avon"—
muddied, I fuppofe, and debafed by the home-bred
ftreamlets of one Shakefpeare.

" In fuller prefence we defcry
Mid mountain rocks—a deity
Than eye of man fhall e'er behold
In living grace of *fculptur'd* gold *

'Tis not enough (though this be fomewhat too,

NOTES.

I would give fomething to know this " learned
gentleman's" idea of fculpturing. In the Regent,
he talks of a " Sculptor's kneading docile clay ! ! !"

More matter for a May morning !

ODE ON APATHY.

" Accurs'd be dull lethargic Apathy,
Whether at eve fhe liftlefs ride
In fluggifh car by tortoife drawn—
With mimic air of fenfelefs pride,

She feebly throws on all her withering fight,
While too obfervant of her fway
Unmark'd her droning fubjects lie,
Alike to her who murmur or obey.

I hope the reader underftands it.

---

* Mr. Parfons fays " thefe lines are not Greathead's."
But they are publifhed with his name in the Album ; which
exclufive of their ftupidity, is fufficient authority for me.
If our doughty critic choofes to take them to himfelf, I can
have no objection ; for, after all, pugna eft de paupere regno!

And more perhaps * than Jerningham can do)

***

NOTES.

ODE TO DUEL.

" Never didſt thou appear
While Tiber's ſons gave law to all the world ;
Yet much they loved to deſolate and ſlaughter,
Carthage atteſt my words
To glut their ſanguinary rage,
Not citizens but gladiators fall.
Slavery and vaſſalage,
And ſavage broils, 'twixt nobles are no more.
Vaniſh thou likewiſe "———

And theſe are ODES, good heavens ! " After the manner of Pindar," I take for granted.

But enough of Mr. G. whom I heſitate not to pronounce, with all his " ſcholarſhip," as ignorant a man as any in the three kingdoms. I have only to add, that I am aſtuated by no perſonal diſlike of Mr. G.; for I can ſay with the greateſt truth (what indeed I can of all the heroes of the Mæviad) that I have not the ſlighteſt knowledge of him. But the daws have ſtrutted too long : it is more than time to ſtrip them of their adventitious plumage ; and if, in doing it, I ſhall pluck off any feathers which originally belonged to them, they have only to thank their own vanity, or the forwardneſs of their injudicious friends.

* And more perhaps than Jerningham can do.—
No ; Mr. Jerningham has lately written a Tragedy

'Tis not enough to dole out Ahs ! and Ohs !

NOTES.

and a Farce; both extremely well fpoken of by
the Reviewers, and both gone to the " paftry-
cooks."

I thought I underftood fomething of faces; but
I muft read my Lavater over again I find. That a
gentleman with the " phyfiognomie d'un mouton
qui rêve," fhould fuddenly ftart forth a new Tyrtæus,
and pour a dreadful note thro' a cracked war-
trump, amazes me—Well; FRONTI NULLA FIDES
fhall henceforth be my motto !

In the pride of his heart Mr. J. has taken the
inftrument from his mouth, and given me a fmart
ftroke on the head with it: this is fair,

Cædimus, inque vicem præbemus crura fagittis.

He has alfo levelled a deadly blow at a gentleman,
who moft affuredly never dreamed of having our
Drawcanfir for an antagonift : this, though not quite
fo fair, is not altogther unprecedented ;

An eagle towering in his pride of place,
Was by a moufing owl hawked at !

There is a trait of fcholarfhip in Mr. Jerningham's
laft poem, which fhould not be overlooked; more

Through Kemble's thorax*, or through Benfley's nofe ;

NOTES.

efpecially as it is the only one. Having occafion to mention " Agave and her *infant* *," he fubjoirs the following explanation : " Alluding to Agave, who in a dilirium flew her *child*. See Ovid." No, I'll take Mr. Jerningham's word for it, though I had twenty Ovids before me.

* Kemble's thorax * * * hiatus valde deflendus * * * But why mention Mr. Benfley ? Why not ? Is not Mr. Benfley a public man, and his fnuffling an objeft of public concern ? But Mr. Benfley is a good man ; and perfeft in every duty of life. I am glad of it from my foul ; and, if I were on the topic of private virtues, would be the firft to praife him. But this is from the purpofe. While I only follow the fair ground of public criticifm, I know of no ftatute, political or moral, which forbids my faying to Mr. Benfley, or any other man whofe nofe I diflike,

————————————— Exi
Jam gravis es nobis, & fæpe emungeris ; Exi
Ocyus & propera————

---

* See his " Peace, Ignominy, and Deftruftion," Page 15.

G

To fill our ftage with fcaffolds, or to fright
Our wives with rapes, repeated thrice a night,
JUDGES——Not fuch as felf-created, fit   35
On that TREMENDOUS BENCH* which fkirts the
  pit,
Where idle Thefpis nods, while Arno† dreams
Of Nereids " purling in ambrofial ftreams ;"   40

NOTES.

* When this was written, (which was while the
Opera Houfe was ufed for plays) the " learned juf-
ticers" here enumerated, together with others *not
yet taken,* were accuftomed to flock nightly to this
BENCH, from which the unlettered vulgar were always fcornfully repelled with an ΟΥΔΕΙΣ. ΑΜΟΥΣΟΣ.

I have not heard whether the New Theatre be
poffeffed of fuch a one : I think not; for critics are
no more gregarious than fpiders. Like them, they
might do great things in concert, but, like them too,
they ufually end with devouring one another.

† Arno. The dreams of this gentleman, which
continue to make their appearance in the Oracle, un-

Where Efte in rapture cons fantaftic airs,

" Old Piftol new-revived" in Topham ftares,

And Bofwell, aping with prepofterous pride

Johnfon's worft frailties, rolls from fide to fide,

His heavy head from hour to hour erects,   45

Affects the fool, and is what he affects *——

JUDGES of truth and fenfe, yet more demand :

That art to nature lend a helping hand !

NOTES.

der the name of Thefpis, are not always of Nereids.
He dreamed one night that Mr. Pope played Pofthu-
mus with lefs fpirit than ufual ; and it was Mr. Johnfon finging Grammachre ! Another night, that the
Mourning Bride might have been better caft, and
lo ! it was the Comedy of Errors that was played ! ! !

This was rather unfortunate : but the reader muft
have already obferved, from the ftrange occupations
of thefe " felf-created judges" (which I have faith-
fully defcribed) that, fleeping or waking, they were
attentive to every thing but what paffed before their
eyes.

* Pauper videri Cotta vult, et eft pauper !

That fables well devifed, be fimply told,
Correct if new, and probable if old.

When Mafon leads Elfrida forth to view,
Adorn'd with virtues which fhe never knew,
I feel for every tear ; while born along
By the full tide of unrefifted fong,
I ftop not to enquire if all be juft,
But take her goodnefs, as her grief, on truft ;
'Till calm reflection checks me, and I fee
The heroine as fhe was, and ought to be,
A bold, bad woman, wading to the throne
Thro' feas of blood, and crimes till then un-
  known :   60
Then, then I hate the magic that deceived,
And blufh to think how fondly I believed *.

NOTES.

* Mr. Parfons' note on this paffage is—" Did
you BELIEVE ! Could you poffibly be fo ignorant ?"—
Even fo. But I humbly conceive Mr. Mafon, who
feduced my unfufpecting youth, is equally culpa-
ble with myfelf. There is alfo one William Shakef-

Not fo, when Atheling*, made in fome strange
    plot
The hero of a day that knew him not,

---

peare, who, I am ready to take my oath, is a no-
torious offender in this way; having led not only
me, but divers others, into the moft grofs and ridiculous errors; making us laugh, cry, and I know
not what, for perfons whom we ought to have known
to be mere non-entities.

But Mr. Parsons has happily obtained an obdu-
rate and impaffible head: let him, therefore, " give
God thanks, and make no boaft of it." He is a wife
and a wary reader, and follows the moft judicious *Bottom*, who, having like himfelf, too much fagacity to
be impofed upon by a feigned charaĉter, was laudably
anxious to undeceive the world. " No," quoth he,
" let him thruft his face through the lion's neck, and
fay, If you think I come hither as a lion, it were
pity of my life——no, I am no fuch thing: I am a
man, as other men are;—and then, indeed, let him
name his name, and tell them plainly that he is SNUG
the joiner."

* Atheling. See the Battle of Haftings. A tragedy in which Mr. Cumberland has contrived with

G 3

Struts from the field his enemy had won,   65

On stately stilts, exulting and undone !

Here I can only pity, only fmile ;

Where not one grace, one elegance of style,

Redeems the audacious folly of the rest,

Truth facrificed, and history made a jest.   70

    Let this, Ye Crufcans*, if your heads be
        made

" Of penetrable stuff," let this perfuade

Your hufky tribes their wanderings to restrain,

Nor hope what taste and Mafon failed to gain:

---

matchlefs dexterity, to introduce every abfurdity of
every kind.

  * Ye Crufcans !

      O voi, che della CRUSCA vi chiamate
      Come quei che farina non avendo
      Di QUELLA a tutto pafto vi faziate !—

Then let your style be brief, your meaning
   clear,   75
Nor, like Lorenzo*, tire the labouring ear
With a wild waste of words; found without
   fenfe,
And all the florid glare of impotence.

IMITATIONS.

V. 75. Eft brevitate opus, ut currat fententia,
   neu fe
Impediat verbis laffas onerantibus aures;
Et fermone opus eft modo trifti fæpe jocofo.

NOTES.

* Lorenzo. " A lamentable tragedy by Della
Crufca, mixed full of pleafant mirth." The
houfe laughed a-good at it; but Mr. Harris
cried fadly. Here is another inftance, if it were
wanted, of the bad effects of proftitute applaufe.
Could this gentleman, if his mind had not been previoufly warped by the eternal puffs of Bell and his
followers, have fuppofed, for a moment, that a
knack of ftringing together " hoar hills" and
" ripling rills," and " red fkies glare" and " thin,
thin air," qualified a man for writing tragedy !

Still with your characters your language change,80
From grave to gay, as nature dictates range ;
Now droop in all the plaintivenefs of woe,
Now in glad numbers light and airy flow,
Now fhake the stage with guilt's alarming tone,
And make the aching bofom all your own ;
Now——But I fing in vain ; from firft to laft, 85
Your joy is fustian, and your grief bombast :
Rhetoric has banifhed reafon ; kings and queens
Vent in hyperboles their royal fpleens ;
Guardfmen in metaphors exprefs their hopes,
And maidens in white linen howl in tropes.   90
Reverent I greet the bards of other days. '
Blest be your names ! and lasting be your praife !
From nature's varied face ye wifely drew,
And following ages owned the copies true.

IMITATIONS.

V. 91. Illi fcripta quibus comœdia prifca
            viris eft
Hoc ftabant, hoc funt imitandi——

O ! had our fots, who rhyme with headlong
    haste,   95

And think reflection still a foe to taste,

But brains your pregnant fcenes to understand,

And give us truth, tho' but at fecond hand,

'Twere fomething yet ! But no; they never
    look——

Shall fouls of fire, they cry, a tutor brook ? 100

Forbid it infpiration ! Thus your pain

Is void, and ye have lived for them in vain ;

In vain for Crufca, and his fkipping fchool,

Cobbe, Reynolds, Andrews, and that Nobler
    Fool ;

IMITATIONS.

V. 103. —— quos neque pulcher
Hermogenes unquam legit, nec fimius ifte,
Nil præter Calvum doctus cantare Catullum.

Who nought but Laura's* tinkling trafh ad-
    mire,   105
And the mad jangle of Matilda's* lyre.

NOTES.

* Laura's tinkling trafh, &c. I had amaffed a
world of this " tinkling trafh" for the behoof of the
reader; but having fortunately for him, miflaid it,
and not being difpofed to undertake again the drud-
gery of wading through Mr. Bell's colleftions, I can
only offer him the little that occurs to my memory.
Of this little, the merits muft be fhared among Mrs.
Robinfon, Mrs. Cowley, and Mr. Merry.

    Et vos, O Lauri, carpam, & te proxima, Myrte,
    Sic pofitæ quoniam fuaves mifcetis odores.

    O let me fly
    Where greenland darknefs drinks the beamy
        fky !

    But oh ! beware how thou doft fling
    Thy *bot pulfe* o'er the quivering ftring ! ! !

      Pluck from their dark and rocky bed
        The yelling demons of the deep,
      Who foaring o'er the comet's head,
        The bofom of the welkin fweep.

But Crufca ftill has merit, and may claim
No humble ftation in the ranks of fame ;

IMITATIONS.

V. 107. At magnum fecit, quod verbis Græca
    Latinis
Mifcuit.

NOTES.

And when the jolly full moon laughs,
In her clear zenith to behold
The envious ftars withdraw their gleams of
    gold,
'Tis to thy health fhe ftooping quaffs
The fapphire cup that fairy zephyrs bring ! ! !

On confidering thefe and the preceding lines, I was
tempted to indulge a wifh that the blue-ftocking club
would iffue an immediate order to Mr. Bell, to examine the cells of Bedlam. Certainly, if an accurate tranfcript were made from the " darken'd walls"
once or twice a quarter, an ALBUM might be prefent-
ed to the fafhionable world, more poetical, and far
more rational, than any they have lately honoured
with their applaufe.

He taught us first the language to refine,

To croud with beauties every fparkling line ; 110

NOTES.

Why does thy ftream of *fweeteft* fong
Foam on the mountain's murmuring fide,
Or through the vocal covert glide!

I heard a tuneful phantom in the wind,
I faw it watch the rifing moon afar
Wet with the weeping of the twilight ftar.——

The pilgrim who with *tearful* eye fhall view
The moon's wan luftre in the midnight dew,
Sooth'd by her light.——

This is an admirable reafon for his crying :—but
what ! Un fot trouve toujours un plus fot qui l'admire.
Mr. Bell is in raptures with it, and very properly
recommends it to the admiration of Merry, as being
the produdtion of " a congenial foul." There is
alfo another judicious critic, one Dr. Tafker (fhould
it not be Dr. Trufler ?) who has given a decided
opinion, it feems, in favour of this lady's abilities;
which may confole her for the fneers of fifty fuch
envious fcribblers as the author of the Baviad.

And firft you fhall hear what Mrs. Robinfon fays
of Dr. Tafker.——" The *learned* and *ingenious* Dr.

Old phrafes with new meanings to difpenfe,

Amufe the fancy, and ——Confound the fenfe :

NOTES.

Tafker, in the third volume of his *elegant* and *cri-tical* works, has PRONOUNCED fome of Mrs. Robin-fon's poems fuperior to thofe of Milton on the fame fubject, particularly her addrefs to the nightingale I The praifes of fo *competent* and *difnterefted* a judge STAMPS celebrity that neither time nor envy can obliterate I I I

Oracle, Dec; 10.

Next you fhall hear what Dr. Tafker fays of Mrs. Robinfon.

" In antient Greece by two fair forms were feen
Wifdom's ftern goddefs, and Love's fmiling queen,
Pallas prefided over arms and arts,
And Venus over gentle virgins' hearts,
But now both powers in one fair form combine,
And in famed Robinfon united fhine.

This lady, equally celebrated in the polite and literary circles, has honoured Mr.—Lo I the Dr. is dwindled into plain Mr.—has honoured Mr. Tafker's poetical and other productions with high and diftin-guifhed marks of her approbation I"

Exeter Paper, Jan. 16.

O, void of reafon ! Is it thus you praife
A linfey-woolfey fong, framed with fuch eafe,

IMITATIONS.

V. 113—116. —— O feri ftudiorum ! quine
putetis
Difficile et mirum, RHODIO quod PITHOLEONTI
Contigit.

NOTES.

Why this is the very fong of Prodicus η χαιρ την
χαιρα κηζει——for the reft, I truft my readers will
readily fubfcribe to the praifes thefe moft " competent and difinterefted judges" have reciprocally la-
vifhed on each other.

But allons,

——My hand at night's fell noon
Plucks from the treffes of the moon
A fparkling crown of filv'ry hue,
Befprent with ftuds of frozen dew !

On the dizzy *beight* inclined
I *liften* to the paffing *wind*
That loves my *mournful fong* to feize,
And bears it to the *mountain breeze.*

Such vacancy of thought, that every line   115
Might tempt e'en VAUGHAN to whifper, " THIS
   is mine!

NOTES.

Here we find that liftening to the wind, and finging to
it are one and the fame thing; and that—but I can
make nothing of the reft.

> When in black obtrufive clouds
> The chilly moon her pale cheek fhrouds,
> I mark the twinkly ftarring train
> Exulting glitter in her wane,
> And proudly gleam their borrowed light
> To gem the fombre dome of night.

What an admirable obferver of nature is this great
poetefs! The ftar *twinkling* in a cloudy night, and
gleaming its BORROWED luftre is fuperlative. I had
almoft forgot to obferve that thefe, and the preceding
lines, are taken from the Ode to the Nightingale; fo
fuperior, in the reverend judgment of Dr. Tafker,
to one of a Mr. John Milton on the fame fubject.

> ——the lightning's rays
> Leap through the night's fcarce pervious gloom,
> Attracted by——(what, for a ducat ?)
> Attracted by the rofes bloom ! ! !

VÁUGHAN! well remembered. He good
man complains
That I affixed his name to Edwin's* ſtrains :

NOTES.

Let but thy lyre impatient ſeize
Departing twilight's filmy breeze,
That winds the inchanting chords among
In lingering labyrinths of ſong.——

See in the clouds its maſt the proud bark laves,
Scorning the aid of ocean's humble waves !

From this it appears that Mrs. Cowley fancies proud
barks float on their maſts. It is proper to mention
that the veſſel takes ſuch extraordinary ſtate on her-
felf, becauſe ſhe carries Della Cruſca !

——— from a young grove's ſhade
Whoſe infant boughs but mock the expeƈting
glade ! ! !
Sweet ſounds ſtole forth, upborn upon the gale,
Prefs'd thro' the air, and broke upon the vale ;

Then ſilent walked the breezes of the plain,
Or ſoared aloft, and ſeiz'd the hovering ſtrain.———
                                        Della Cruſca.

The force of folly can no farther go !

'Tis juft—for what three kindred fouls have
    done,
Is most unfairly charged, I ween, on one.   120
Pardon, my learned friend! With wat'ry eyes
Thy growing fame to truth I facrifice ;

NÒTES.

* Edwin's ſtrains. If the reader will turn to the
conclufion of the Baviad, he will find a delicious
Επιταφιον on a tame moufe, by this learned gentleman. As it feemed to give univerfal fatisfaction, I
embrace with pleafure the opportunity of laying
before him another effufion of the fame exquifite
pen.

It will be found, I flatter myfelf, not lefs beautiful than the former, and will ferve admirably to
prove that the author, though oftenfibly devoted
to Elegy, can, on a proper occafion, affume an air
of gaiety, and be " profound" with eafe, and in-
ftructive with elegance.

Εδουιν προλογιζιι.

" On the circumftance of a maftiff's running fu-
rioufly fad dog! towards two young ladies, and
upon coming up to them, becoming inftantly gentle
good dog! and tractable."

H

To many a fonnet call thy claims in doubt,

And "at one entrance fhut thy glory out."

Yet MEWL thou still. Shall my lord's dor-

  moufe die,   125

And low in dust without a requiem lie!

No, MEWL thou still: and while thy d‑ ‑ 's join,

Their melancholy fymphonies to thine,

NOTES.

Tantum ad narrandum argumentum eft benignitas.

" When Orpheus took his *lyre* to hell
 To fetch his rib away,
On that fame thing he pleas'd fo well,
 That devils learn'd to play.

Befides in books it may be read,
 That whilft he fwept the *lute*
Grim Cerb'rus hung his favage head,
 And lay aftoundly mute.

But here we can with juftice fay
 That nature rivals art,

My righteous verfe fhall labour to reſtore

The well-earned fame it robbed them of be-

    fore.   130

EDWIN, whatever elegies of woe

Drop from the gentle mouths of Vaughan and

    Co.

To this or that, henceforth no more confined,

Shall, like a furname, take in all the kind.

    Right! cry the brethren. When the heaven-

    born mufe   135

Shames her defcent, and for low earthly views,

Hums o'er a beetle's bier the doleful ſtave,

Or fits chief mourner at a May-bug's grave,

Satire fhould fcourge her from the vile employ,

And bring her back to friendfhip, love, and

    joy.   140

NOTES.

    He *ſang* a maſtiff's rage away,
      You look'd one thro' the heart."

                          Fecit EDWIN.

H 2

But fpare Cefario[1], Carlos , Adelaide[3],

---

[1] Cefario. In the Baviad (p. 48) there are a few ftanzas of a moft deleftable ode to an owl. They were afcribed to Arno : nor was I confcious of any miftake, 'till I received a polite note from that gentleman, affuring me that he was not only not the author of them; but (horefco referens) that he thought them "execrable." Mr. Bell, on the other hand, affirms them to be " admirable."

Who fhall decide when doftors difagree ?

Be this as it may, I am happy to fay that I have difcovered the true author. They were written by Cefario; and as I rather incline to Mr. Bell, pace Arnò dixerim, I fhall make no fcruple of laying the remainder of this " mellifluous piece" before my reader.

" Slighted love the *foul* fubduing,
   Silent forrow *chills* the *heart*,
Treach'rous fancy ftill *purfuing*,
   Still *repels* the *poifoned* dart.

Soothing thofe fond *dreams* of pleafure
   Pictur'd in the *glowing* breaft,
Lavifh of her fweeteft *treafure*
   Anxious *fear* is *charm'd* to *reft.*——

The truest poetefs! the truest maid!

NOTES.

Fearlefs o'er the whiten'd *billows*,
Proudly rife, fweet bird of night,
Safely through the bending *willows*
Gently wing thy *aery* flight.

CESARIO.

Though I flatter myfelf I have good fenfe and tafte enough to fee, and admire the peculiar beauties of this ode, yet a regard for truth obliges me to declare they are not original. They are taken (with improvements, I confefs) from a moft beautiful "fong by a perfon of quality," in Pope's Mifcellanies. This, though it detracts a little from Cefario's inventive powers, ftill leaves him the praife (no mean one) of having gone beyond that great poet, in what he probably confidered as the ne plus ultra of ingenuity.

Venimus ad fummum fortunæ! Mr. Greathead equals Shakefpeare, Mrs. Robinfon furpaffes Milton, and Cefario outdoes Pope in that very performance, which he vainly imagined fo complete as to take away all defire of imitating, all poffibility of excelling it!

O favoured clime! O happy age!

H 3

Lorenzo[4], Rueben[5], fpare : far be the thought

NOTES.

[2] Carlos. I have nothing of this gentleman (a moft pertinacious fcribbler in the Oracle) but the following " fonnet;" luckily, however, it is fo ineffably ftupid, that it will more than fatisfy any reader but Mr. Bell's.

ON A LADY'S PORTRAIT.

Oft hath the poet hailed the breath of morn,
   That wakens nature with the voice of fpring,
And oft, when purple fummer feeds the lawn,
   Hath fancy touched him with her procreant wing,
Full frequent has he blefs'd the golden beam
   Which yellow autumn glowing fpreads around,
And tho' pale winter prefl'd a paly gleam,
   Frefh in his breaft was young defcription found——

I can copy no more—Job himfelf would lofe all patience here. Inftead, therefore, of the remainder of this incomprehenfible trafh, I will give the reader a ftring of judicious obfervations by Mr. T. Vaughan. " Bruyere fays, he will allow that good writers are fcarce enough, but adds, and juftly, that good critics are equally fo : which *reminds our correfpondent* alfo of what the Abbé Trublet *writes, fpeaking* of profeffed critics,

Of intereſt, far from them. Unbribed, unbought,

---

where he *ſays*, if they were obliged to examine authors impartially——there would be fewer writers in
this way. Was this to be the liberal practice adopted
by our modern critics, we ſhould not ſee a BAVIAD
—(Oons! who is this BAVIAD!)—falling upon men
and things, that are much above his capacity, and
ſeemingly for no other reaſon than becauſe they
are ſo."

A Daniel come to judgment, yea, a Daniel! This
is in truth the reaſon ; and when Mr. Vaughan and his
coadjutors will condeſcend to humble themſelves to
my underſtanding, I will endeavour to profit by their
eloquent ſtrictures.

³ Adelaide. And who is Adelaide? O ſeri ſtudio-
rum! " Not to know her argues yourſelves unknown." Hear Mr. Bell, the Longinus of Newſ-
paper writers.

ADELAIDE.

" HE who is here addreſſed by the firſt lyric writer
in the kingdom, muſt himſelf endeavour to repay a
debt ſo highly honourable, if it can be done by verſe!
This Lady ſhall have the praiſe, which ought to be

H 4

They pour * from their big breast's prolific zone,

---

given by the COUNTRY ! ! ! that of firſt diſcovering, and drawing out the *fine powers* of Arno and Della Cruſca !"

" O thou whom late I watch'd while o'er thee hung
The orb, whoſe glories I ſo oft have ſung,
Beheld thee while a *ſhower of beam*
Made night a lovelier morning ſeem," &c.

We might here diſmiſs this " firſt lyric writer of the age," who, from her flippant nonſenſe, appears to be Mrs. Piozzi ; were it not for the ſake of remark-ing, that whatever be the merit of " drawing out the fine powers of Arno" (which, it ſeems this ungrateful country has not yet rewarded with a ſtatue) ſhe muſt be content to ſhare it with Julia. Hear her Invoca-tion—but firſt hear Mr. Bell. " A moſt elegant com-pliment, which for generous eſteem has been ſeldom equalled, any more than the muſe which inſpired it."

JULIA TO ARNO.

Arno ! where ſteals thy dulcet lay
    Soft as the evening's minſtrel note,
Say, does it deck the riſing day,
    Or on the noon-tide breezes float ! ! !

A proud, poetic fervour, only known

Mrs. Robinſon (for we may as well drop the name
of Julia) has been guilty of a trifling larceny here;
having taken from the Baviad without any ac-
knowledgment, a delicious couplet which I flat-
tered myſelf would never have been ſeen out of
that poem——but ſo it is, that, like Pope,

—— write whate'er I will,
Some riſing genius SINS up to it ſtill.

This has nettled me a little, and poſſibly injured
the great poeteſs in my opinion; for I have been
robbed ſo often of late, that I begin to think with
the old œconomiſt,

Ουτ Θ- αοιδων λωϛ Θ- οϛ ιξ εμευ οισεται ɤδεν.

For the reſt, this "Invocation" called forth a
ſpecimen of Arno's fine powers in the following
dulcet lays.

ARNO TO JULIA.

Sure ſome dire ſtar inimical to man
 Guides to his heart the deſolating fire,
Fills with contention only his brief ſpan,
 And rouzes him to murderous deſire.

To fouls like theirs' ; as Anna's youth infpires,

NOTES.

'There are who fagely fcan the tortured world,
    And tell us war is but neceffity,
That millions, by the great difpenfer hurl'd,
    Muft fuffer by this fcourge, and ceafe to be.

Euge Poeta !

⁴ Lorenzo. Και πως εγω Σθενελϖ φαγοιμ'αι ρημα τι
    Εις οξ◯ εμϐαπ7ομενον, η λευκϖς αλας——

Says a hungry wight in an old comedy. But I know
of no feafoning, whatever, capable of making the
infipid garbage of this modern Sthenelus palatable,
even to the voracious appetite of the blue-ftocking
club : I fhall therefore fpare myfelf the difguft of
producing it.

⁵ Reuben, whom I take to be Mr. Greathead in
difguife, (it being this gentleman's fate, like Hercules
of old, to affume the merit of all unappropriated
prodigies) Reuben introduced himfelf to the WORLD
by the following " Addrefs to Anna Matilda." .

As Laura's graces kindle fierce defires,

NOTES.

To thee a ftranger dares addrefs his theme,
   To thee, proud miftrefs of Apollo's lyre,
One ray emitted from thy golden gleam,
   Prompted by love would fet the world on fire!
Adorn then love in fancy–tinctured veft,
   Camelion like, anon of various hue,
By Penferofo, and Allegro dreft,
   Such genius claim'd when fhe Idalia drew.——

   Anna Matilda, what could fhe lefs! found

      ——— this refufcitating praife
   Breathe life upon her dying lays,

Like " the daify which fpreads her bloom to the
moift evening "!!! and accordingly produced a
matchlefs " adornment of love," to the great con-
tentment of the gentle Reuben.

   But bard polite, quoth fhe, how hard the tafk
   Which with *fuch elegance* you afk!

Who could have thought thefe lines, the fimple
tribute of gratitude to genius, would have nearly
occafioned " a perdition of fouls!" Yet fo it was.
They unfortunately rouzed the jealoufy of Della

As Henriett——For heaven's fake! not fo faft.

I too, my mafters, ere my teeth were caft,   150

NOTES:

Crufca " on the fportive banks of the Rhone."—
One lucklefs evening

> " When twilight on the weftern edge
> Had twined his hoary hair with fabling fedge,"

as he was " weeping" (for, like Mafter Stephen, thefe
good creatures think it neceffary to be always melancholy) at the tomb of Laura, he ftarted, as well he
might, at the accurfed name of Reuben.

> Hark! quoth he,
> What cruel founds are thefe
> Which float upon the languid breeze,
> Which fill my foul with jealous fear!
> Hah! REUBEN is the name I hear.
> For him my *faithlefs* Anna, &c.

It is with no fmall regret I add, that the cold-
blooded Bell has deftroyed this beautiful fancy-fcene
with one ftroke of his clownifh pen.   In a note on the
above lines (Album, p. 134) he officioufly informs us
that Della Crufca knew " nothing of his rival, till
he READ" detefted word! " his fonnet in the Oracle."   O Bell! Bell! Is it thus thou humbleft the
ftrains of the fublime! Surely we may fay of thee
what was not ill faid of one of thy fifters,

Had learned, by rote, to rave of Dèlia's charms,

To die of tranſports found in Chloe's arms,

Coy Daphne with obstreperous plaints to woo,

And curſe the cruelty of——God knows who.

IMITATIONS.

V. 150. Atqui Ego cum græcos facerem, na-
tus mare citra,

Verſiculos, vetuit tali me voce Quirinus

Poſt mediam viſus noctem, cum ſomnia vera.

NOTES.

Sed tu inſulſa male et moleſta vives,
Per quam non licet eſſe negligentem.

* They pour, &c.

————I love ſo well
Thy ſoul's deep tone, thy thought's high ſwell,
Thy proud poetic fervour known,
But in thy breaſt's prolific zone.

Dell. Cruſ.

When Phœbus, (not the Power that bade thee
      write,   155

For he, dear Dapper! was a lying fprite)

One morn, when dreams are true, approached my
      fide,

And, frowning on my tuneful lumber, cried,

" Lo! every corner with foft fonnets crammed,

And high-born odes, " works damned, or to be
      damned :"   160

And is THY active folly adding more

To this most worthlefs, moft fuperfluous ftore ?

O impotence of toil ! thou mighteft as well

Give fenfe to Efte, or modefty to Bell.

Forbear, forbear: what tho' thou canft not
      claim   165

The facred honours of a POET's name,

Due to the few alone, whom I infpire

With lofty rapture, with etherial fire !

Yet mayft thou arrogate the humble praife

Of reafon's bard, if, in thy future lays,   170

Plain fenfe, and truth, (and furely thefe are
 thine)

Correct thy wanderings, and thy flights confine."

Here ceafed the God, and vanifhed. Forth I
 fprang

While in my ear the voice divine yet rang ;

Seized every rag and fcrap, approached the
 fire,   175

And faw whole ALBUMS in the blaze expire.

 Then fhame enfued, and vain regret, to have
 fpent

So many hours (hours which I yet lament,)

In thriftlefs induftry ; and year on year

Inglorious rolled, while diffidence, and fear, 180

Repreft my voice——unheard till ANNA came,

What ! throbb'st thou YET, my bofom, at the
 name ?

And chafed the oppreffive doubts that round me
 clung,

And fired my breast, and loofened all my tongue.

E'en then (admire, John Bell! my fimple
     ways)   185
No heaven, and hell, danced madly thro' my
     lays,
No oaths, no execrations ; all was plain :
Yet, truft me, while thy " ever jingling train"
Chime their fonorous woes with frigid art,
And fhock the reafon and revolt the heart ;   190
My hopes, and fears, in nature's language drest,
Awakened love in many a gentle breast.

   How oft, O DART! what time the faithful
     pair
Walked forth, the fragrant hour of eve to fhare,
On thy romantic banks, have my wild ftrains*, 195
(Not yet forgot amidst my native plains)

IMITATIONS.

V. 195. In fylvam non ligna feras infaniùs,
    ac fi

Magnas Græcorum malis implere catervas——

* Mr. Parfons is extremely angry at my " oftentatious intrufion" of the " Otium Divos" into the

T. Stothard R.A del.   A. Birrell sculp.

Hence! in the name — I scarce had spoke, when lo!
Reams of outrageous sonnets, thick as snow,
Flew round my head; yet, in my cause secure,
"Pour on," I cried, "pour on, I will endure." —

Mæviad. line 271.

Published July 15. 1797. by J. Wright, Piccadilly.

While THOU hast fweetly gurgled down the vale,
Filled up the paufe of love's delightful tale!

NOTES.

notes on this poem.   What could I do?   I ever
difliked publifhing my little modicums on loofe pages
—but I fhall grow wifer by his example; and, indeed,
am even now compofing " one Riddle, two Rebuffes,
and an Acroftic, to a child at nurfe,*" which will
be fet forth with all convenient·fpeed.   Meanwhile
I am tempted to offend once more, and fubjoin the
only two of my " wild ftrains" that now live in
my recollection.   I can affure Mr. P. they were
written on the occafions they profefs to be—and the
laft of them at a time when I had no idea of fur-
viving to provoke his indignation:

> ——— fed Cynaræ breves
> Annos fata dederunt, me
> · Servatura diu.

TO A TUFT OF EARLY VIOLETS.

Sweet flowers! that from your humble beds
    Thus prematurely dare to rife,
And truft your unprotected heads
    To cold Aquarius' watry fkies;

---

* See " ONE Epigram, Two Sonnets, and ONE Ode to
a Boy at School, by W. Parfons, Efq."

I

While, ever as fhe read, the confcious maid,

By faultering voice, and downcast looks betray'd   200

NOTES.

Retire, retire! THESE tepid airs
  Are not the genial brood of May;
THAT fun with light malignant glares,
  And flatters only to betray.

Stern Winter's reign is not yet paft——
  Lo! while your buds prepare to blow,
On icy pinions come's the blaft,
  And nips your root, and lays you low.

Alas, for fuch ungentle doom!
  But I will fhield you; and fupply
A kindlier foil on which to bloom,
  A nobler bed on which to die.

Come then—ere yet the morning ray
  Has drunk the dew that gems your creft,
And drawn your balmieft fweets away;
  O come, and grace my ANNA's breaft.

Ye droop, fond flowers! But, did ye know
  What worth, what goodnefs there refide,
Your cups with livelieft tints would glow,
  And fpread their leaves with confcious pride.

Would blufhing on her lover's neck recline,

And with her finger—point the tenderest line.

NOTES.

For there has liberal Nature join'd
  Her riches to the ftores of Art,
And added to the vigorous mind,
  The foft, the fympathizing heart.

Come then—ere yet the morning ray
  Has drunk the dew that gems your creft,
And drawn your balmieft fweets away ;
  O come and grace my ANNA's breaft.

O! I fhould think,—that fragrant bed
  Might I but hope with you to fhare,—
Years of anxiety repaid,
  By one fhort hour of tranfport there.

More bleft than me, thus fhall ye live
  Your little day ; and when ye die,
Sweet flowers ! the grateful mufe fhall give
  A verfe ; the forrowing maid, a figh.

While I alas ! no diftant date,
  Mix with the duft from whence I came,
Without a friend to weep my fate,
  Without a ftone to tell my name.

I 2

But thefe are paft : and, mark me, Laura!

time

That made what then was venial, now a crime,

NOTES.

WRITTEN TWO YEARS AFTER THE PRECEDING.

I wifh I was where ANNA lies ;
   For I am fick of lingering here
And every hour Affection cries,
   Go, and partake her humble bier.

I wifh I could ! For when fhe died
   I loft my all ; and life has prov'd
Since that fad hour a dreary void,
   A wafte unlovely, and unlov'd.—

But who, when I am turn'd to clay,
   Shall duly to her grave repair,
And pluck the ragged mofs away,
   And weeds that have " no bufinefs there ?"

And who with pious hand fhall bring
   The flowers fhe cherifh'd, fnow-drops cold,
And violets that unheeded fpring,
   To fcatter o'er her hallow'd mold ?

To more befitting cares my thoughts confined, 205
And drove with youth, its follies from my mind.

NOTES.

And who, while memory loves to dwell
 Upon her name for ever dear,
Shall feel his heart with paſſion ſwell,
 And pour the bitter, bitter tear ?

I DID IT; and would fate allow,
 Should viſit ſtill, ſhould ſtill deplore—
But health and ſtrength have left me now,
 And I alas! can weep no more.

Take then, ſweet maid! this ſimple ſtrain,
 The laſt I offer at thy ſhrine ;
Thy grave muſt then undeck'd remain,
 And all thy memory fade with mine.

And can thy ſoft perſuaſive look,
 Thy voice that might with muſic vie,
Thy air, that every gazer took,
 Thy matchleſs eloquence of eye,

Thy ſpirits, frolickſome, as good,
 Thy courage, by no ills diſmay'd,
Thy patience, by no wrongs ſubdu'd,
 Thy gay good-humour—Can they " fade!"

I 3

Since then, while Merry, and his nurfelings die,
Thrill'd * by the liquid peril of an eye;

IMITATIONS.

V. 207. Turgidus Alpinus jugulat dum
Memnona, dumque
Diffingit Rheni luteum caput, hæc ego ludo,
Quæ nec in æde fonent certantia, judice Tarpâ.—

NOTES.

Perhaps—but forrow dims my eye :
　Cold turf, which I no more muft view,
Dear name, which I no more muft figh,
　A long, a laft, a fad adieu !

* Thrilled, &c.

　　Bid the ftreamy lightnings fly,
　　In liquid peril from thy eye.
　　　　　　　　　　　Dell. Crus.

　　Ne'er fhalt thou know to figh,
　　Or on a foft idea die,
　　Ne'er on a recolleftion gafp,
　　Thy arms——Ohe ! jam fatis eft.
　　　　　　　　　　　Anna Mat.

Gafp at a recollection, and drop down
At the long ftreamy lightning of a frown ; 210
I footh, as humour prompts, my idle vein
In frolick verfe, that cannot hope to gain
Admiffion to the Album, nor be feen
In L——'s Review, or Urban's Magazine.
 O, for thy fpirit, Pope! Yet why? My
  lays, 215
That wake no envy, and invite no praife,
Half-creeping, and half-flying, yet fuffice
To ftagger impudence, and ruffle vice.
An hour may come, fo I delight to dream,
When flowly wandering by thy facred ftream, 220
Majeftic Thames ! I leave the world behind,
And give to fancy all th' enraptur'd mind.
An hour may come, when I fhall ftrike the lyre
To nobler themes : then, then, the chords infpire
With thy own harmony, moft fweet, moft
  ftrong, 225
And guide my hand thro' all the maze of fong !
Till then, enough for me, in fuch rude ftrains
As mother Wit can give, and thofe fmall pains

A vacant hour allows ; to range the town,
And hunt the clamorous brood of Folly down ; 230
Force every head, in Efte's defpite, to wear
The cap and bells, by nature planted there,
Muffle the rattle, feize the flavering fholes,
And drive them, fcourged and whimpering, to
  their holes.

 Burgoyne*, perhaps, unchill'd by creeping
  age,   235
May yet arife, and vindicate the ftage ;
The reign of nature and of fenfe reftore,
And be whatever Terence was before.

IMITATIONS.

 V. 235. Arguta meretrice potes, Davoque
  Chremeta
Eludente fenem, comis garrire libellos
Unus vivorum, Fundani.——

 * Burgoyne. See the note on v. 21.

And you, too, whole Menander! who combine
With his pure language and his flowing line, 240
The SOUL of Comedy ; may steal an hour
From the fond chace of still-escaping power,
The poet and the sage again unite,
And sweetly blend instruction with delight.

And yet Elfrida's bard, tho' time has shed 245
The snow of age too deep around his head ;
Feels the kind warmth, the fervour, that inspired
His youthful breast, still glow unchecked, un-
    tired :
And yet, tho' like the bird of eve, his song
" Fit audience finds" not in the giddy throng ; 250
The notes, tho' artful wild, tho' numerous chaste,
Fill with delight the sober ease of taste,

But these, and more I could with honour name,
Too proud to stoop, like me, to vulgar game,

IMITATIONS.

V. 245. ——molle atque facetum
Virgilio annuerunt gaudentes rure Camenæ.

Subjects more worthy of their daring chufe,   255
And leave at large the abortions of the mufe.
Proud of their privilege, the innumerous fpawn,
From bogs and fens, the mire of Pindus drawn,
New vigour feel, new confidence affume,
And fwarm like Pharaoh's frogs in every room. 260
    Sick of th' eternal croak which, ever near,
Beat like the death-watch on my tortured ear ;
And fure, too fure, that many a genuine child
Of truth and nature, checked his wood-notes
        wild*,

NOTES.

* Checked his wood-notes wild. Σιωπησαίων κολοιων
ασονται κυκνοι. But this is better illuftrated in a moft
elegant fable of Leffing's, to which I defpair of doing
juftice in a tranflation.

    Du zürneft, Liebling der Mufen, &c. &c.

    Thou art troubled, darling of the Mufes, thou art
troubled at the clamorous fwarms of infects which
infeft Parnaffus. O hear from me what once the
nightingale heard from the fhepherd.

Dear to the feeling heart——in doubt to win 265

The vacant wanderer, midst th' unceafing din

Of this hoarfe rout ; I feized at length the wand;

Refolved, tho' fmall my fkill, tho' weak my
    hand,

The mifchief in its progrefs to arrest,

And exorcife the foil of fuch a pest.   270

  Hence ! in the name——I fcarce had fpoke,
      when lo !

Reams of outrageous fonnets *, thick as fnow,

Sing then, faid he to the filent fongftrefs, one lovely evening in the fpring, fing then, fweet nightingale ! Alas ! faid the nightingale, the frogs croak fo loud, that I have loft all defire to fing : doft thou not hear them ? I do, indeed, replied the fhepherd—but thy filence alone is the caufe of it.

  " There's comfort yet !"

  * Reams of outrageous fonnets. Of thefe I have collected a very reafonable quantity, which I purpofe

Flew round my head ; yet, in my caufe fecure

" Pour on," I cried, " pour on, I will endure."—

NOTES.

to prefix to fome future edition of the Mæviad, under
the true claffic head of

INSIGNIUM VIRORUM

ALIQUOT TESTIMONIA

QUI

BAV : ET MÆV : INCLYTISS : AUCTORIS

MEMINERUNT.

Meanwhile I fhall prefent the reader with the two firft
that occur, as a fpecimen of the collection.

SONNET I.

" To the anonymous author of the Baviad, occafioned by his fcurrilous, and moft unmerited attack
on Mr. Wefton.

DEMON OF DARKNESS! whofoe'er thou art,
  That dar'ft affume the brighter angel's form,
And o'er the peaceful vale impel the ftorm,   ·
  With many a figh to rend the *boneft* heart,

What! fhall I fhrink, becaufe the noble
train   275
Whofe judgement I impugn, whofe tafte arraign,

NOTES.

Force from th' *unconfcious* eye the tear to ftart,
  And with juft *pride* th' indignant bofom warm ;
Avaunt ! to where unnumber'd fpirits fwarm,
  Foul and malignant as thyfelf, depart.
Genius of Pope defcend, ye fervile crew
  Of imitators vile, intrude not ! ! !   I appeal
To thee, and thee alone from outrage bafe,
  Tell me tho' fair the forms his fancy drew,
Should'ft thou the fecrets of his heart reveal,
Would fame his memory crown, or cover with dif-
    grace."
                                        J. M.
                  Gent. Mag. Aug. 1792.

This poor driveller, who is ftupid enough to be
Wefton's admirer, and malignant enough to be his
friend, I take to be one Morley;* whom I now and

---

* I was right. Mr. Morley, who I underftand is a clergy-
man, and who, like Mr. Parfons, exults in the idea of having

Alive, and trembling for their favourites' fate,
Purfue my verfe, with unrelenting hate !

NOTES.

then obferve in the Gent. Mag. ufhering his great

---

firft attacked me, has fince publifhed a " TALE," the wit,
or rather dullnefs of which, if I recollect right, confifts in
my being difappointed of a Living !

Here follow a few of the introductory lines which for
poetry and pleafantry can only be exceeded by fome of Mr.
Parfon's.

" What if a little once I did abufe thee ?
" Worfe than thou hadft deferved I could not ufe thee.
" For when I fpied thy Satyr's cloven foot,
" 'Tis very true, I took thee for a brute ;
" And marking more attentively thy manners,
" I fince have wifhed thy hide were at the tanner's.
" But if a man thou art, as fome fuppofe,
" Oh ! how my fingers itch to pull thy nofe !
" As pleafed as Punch, I'd hold it in my gripe,
" Till Parkinfon had ftuffed thee for a fnipe ! ! !

It is rather fingular that this ftill-born lump of infipidity
fhould be iutroduced to the Bookfeller under the aufpices of
DOCTOR PARR. If that refpectable name was not abufed

No :——fave me from their PRAISE, and I can fit
Calm, unconcerned, the butt of Andrew's wit, 280
And Topham's fenfe ; perverfely gay, can fmile
While Efte, the zany, in his motley ftyle,

---

prototype's doggrel into notice, with an importance
truly worthy of it.

SONNET II.

To the execrable Baviad.

MONSTER OF TURPITUDE! who feem'ft inclined
Through me to pierce with thy *impregnate* dart,

---

on the occafion, I can only fay that politics, like mifery,
" bring a man acquainted with ftrange bedfellows"!
For the reft, I will prefent Mr. Morley with a couple of
lines, which, if he will get conftrued and ferioufly refleft
upon, before he next puts pen to paper, may be of more
fervice to him, than all the inftruction, and all the encouragement, the Doctor, apparently, ever gave him :

Cur ego laborem notus effe tam pravè
Cum ftare gratis cum filentio poffim!

Calls barbarous names; while Bell and Boaden
    rave,
And Vaughan, a brother blockhead's verfe to
    fave,

IMITATIONS.

V. 283—288. Men' moveat cimex Pantilius?
    aut crucier, quod
Vellicet abfentem Demetrius? aut quod ineptus
Fannius Hermoginis lædat conviva Tigelli?

NOTES.

The *fine-fpun* NERVE of each *full bofom'd* mind,*
  And rock in *apathy*—the SENSIVE heart,
TREMBLE! for lo! MY ORACLE——*fo famed*
  Shall RING each morn in thy ACCURSED ear
A *griding* pang! so——when the GRECIAN MARE†
  Enter'd the *town*, old Pyramus exclaim'd

---

  * Quere full-bottom'd?   Printer's Devil.
  † Grecian MARE. This has been *hitherto*, inaccurately
enough, named the Trojan HORSE; and, indeed, I myfelf
had nearly fallen into the unfcholarlike error, when my

Toils day by day my character to draw,   285
And heaps upon me every thing—but law.

NOTES.

I fee! I fee!——and *hurl'd* his LIGHTNING fpear,
  While Capaneus drew back HIS head—for fear,
And *godlike** Alexander——gazing round,
  Unconfcious of his victories—TO COME,
Approach'd the monarch, and with *fobs* profound
  Explain'd th' *impending* wrath o'er Ilium's royal
    dome.
                    J. Bell.

---

learned friend Greathead convinced me (from Pope's emen-
dations of Virgil, under the fantaftic name of Scriblerus)
that the animal in queftion was a MARE——She being *there*
faid to be fœta armis, armed with a fœtus. Let us hear no
more, therefore of the Trojan HORSE.

  The patronymick TROJAN is ftill more abfurd. Homer
exprefsly declares the Mare to have been produced by Pallas—Palladis arte : now Pallas was a GRECIAN Goddefs, as
is fufficiently manifeft from her name, which is derived from
Παλλω vibro.
                    J. Bell.

  * Godlike ; that is, Θεοειδης, from Θεο, God, and ειδης,
like. (Vide Hom.) Tranflators in general (I except a late

                K

But do I then, (abjuring every aim)

All cenfure flight, and all applaufe difclaim ?

Not fo : where judgment holds the rod, I bow

My humbled neck, awed by her angry brow ; 290

Where tafte and fenfe approve, I feel a joy

Dear to my heart, and mixed with no alloy.

I write not to the modifh herd : my days,

Spent in the tranquil fhades of letter'd eafe,

Afk no admiring stare from thofe I meet,   295

No loud " that's HE !" to make their paffage

    fweet.

óne) are too inattentive to the compound epithets of this great poet. By why does Homer call Alexander Godlike, when he appears from Curtius Quintiufes tedious gazette, in verfe, to have had one fhoulder higher than the other ? My friend V——thinks it was purely to pay his court to him, in hopes of getting into his Will, or rather *into his* MISTRESSES. It may be fo ; but 'tis ftrange the abfurdity was never noticed before.

Pleafed to steal foftly by, unmarked, unknown,
I leave the world to Holcroft, Pratt *, and
Vaughan.

---

* PRATT. This gentleman lately put in practice a
very notable fcheme. Having fcribbled himfelf fairly
out of notice, he found it expedient to retire to the
continent for a few months—to provoke the enqui-
ries of Mr. Lane's indefatigable readers.

Mark the ingratitude of the creatures! No en-
quiries were made, and Mr. Pratt was forgotten before he had croffed the channel. Ibi omnis effufus
labor.—But what!

The moufe that is content with one poor hole,
Can never be a moufe of any foul.

Baffled in this expedient, he had recourfe to another,
and, while we were dreaming of nothing lefs, came
before us in the following paragraph.

" A few days fince died, at Bafle in Swifferland,
the ingenious Mr. Pratt. His lofs will be feverely
felt by the literary world; as he joined to the ac-
complifhments of the gentleman the erudition of the
fcholar."

K 2

Of thefe enough. Yet may the few I love,

For who would fing in vain! my verfe ap-

prove;   300

Chief thou, my friend! who, from my earliest

years,

Hast fhared my joys, and more than fhared my

cares.

IMITATIONS.

V. 300. —— probat hæc Octavius, optimus

atque

Fufcus: & hæc utinam Vifcorum laudet uterque!

NOTES.

This was inferted in the London papers for feveral days fucceffively. The country papers too "yelled out like fyllables of dolour." At length, while our eyes were yet wet for the irreparable lofs we had fuftained, came a fecond paragraph as follows.

Sure, if our fates hang on fome hidden Power,

And take their colour from the natal hour,

Then, IRELAND *! the fame planet on us

    rofe;   305

Such the strong fympathies our lives difclofe !

NOTES.

" As no event of late has caufed a more general forrow than the fuppofed death of the ingenious Mr. Pratt ; we are happy to have it in our power to affure his numerous admirers, that he is as well as they can wifh, and (what they will be delighted to hear) bufied in preparing his TRAVELS for the prefs."

" Laud we the Gods !"

* Here, on account of its conneftion with the perfon mentioned in the text, I fhall take the liberty—extremum hunc mihi concede of inferting the following " Imitation," addreffed to him feveral years fince. It was never printed : nor, as far as I know, feen by any but himfelf : and I tranfcribe it for the prefs, with mingled fenfations of gratitude and delight, at the favourable change of circumftances we have BOTH experienced fince it was written.

Thou knowest how foon we felt this influence
bland,
And fought the brook and coppice hand in hand,

NOTES.

TO THE
REV. JOHN IRELAND.*

IMITATION OF HORACE.

LIB. II. ODE 16.

Otium Divos rogat, &c.

WHEN howling winds, and louring fkies,
The light, untimber'd bark furprife
   Near Orkney's boifterous feas ;
The trembling crew forget to fwear,
And bend the knees, unufed to prayer,
   To afk a little eafe.

For eafe the Turk, ferocious, prays,
   For eafe the barbarous Ruffe——for eafe,
     Which P——k could ne'er obtain ;
Which Bedford lack'd amidft his ftore,
And liberal Clive, with mines of ore,
   Oft bade for—but in vain.

* Now Vicar of Croydon in Surry, and Author of
" *Difcourfes on the Rejection of the Gofpel by the Antient
Jews and Greeks.*"

And fhaped rude bows, and uncouth whistles
 blew,
And paper kites (a last, great effort,) flew; 310

For not the liveried troop that wait
Around the manfions of the great,
 Can keep, my friend, aloof;
Fear, that attacks the mind by fits,
And Care, that like a raven flits
 Around the lordly roof.

" O, well is he" to whom kind heaven
A decent competence has given!
 Rich in the blefling fent;
He grafps not anxioufly at more,
Dreads not to ufe his little ftore,
 And fattens on content.

" O well is he!" for life is loft,
Amidft a whirl of paffions toft;
 Then why, dear Jack, fhould man,
Magnanimous Ephemera! ftretch
His views beyond the narrow reach
 Of his contracted fpan!

Why fhould he from his country run,
In hopes, beneath a foreign fun,

And when the day was done, retired to rest,
Sleep on our eyes, and funfhine in our breast.

NOTES.

Serener hours to find ?
Was never man in this wild chace,
Who changed his nature with his place,
    And left himfelf behind.

For, winged with all the lightning's fpeed,
Care climbs the bark, Care mounts the fteed,
    An inmate of the breaft:
Nor Barca's heat, nor Zembla's cold,
Can drive from that pernicious hold,
    The too-tenacious gueft.

They, whom no anxious thoughts annoy,
Grateful, the *prefent* hour enjoy,
    Nor feek the *next* to know ;
To lighten every ill they ftrive,
Nor, ere Misfortune's hand arrive,
    Anticipate the blow.

Something muft ever be amifs——
Man has HIS JOYS; but perfect blifs

In riper years, again together thrown,
Our studies, as our ſports before, were one.

NOTES.

Lives only in the brain:
We cannot all have all we want;
And Chance, unaſked, to THIS may grant
    What THAT has begg'd in vain.

WOLF ruſhed on death in manhood's bloom,
PAULET crept ſlowly to the tomb;
    Here breath, *there* fame was given:
And that wiſe Power who weighs our lives,
By *contras*, and by *pros*,* contrives
    To keep the balance even.

---

* In the earlier editions of this poem (which were printed
during my abſence from town) there was an enormous
hallucination in this place—no leſs than a tranſpoſition of
an R! This very naturally called forth all the indignation
of the lynx-eyed and learned Mr. Parſons, and he comment-
ed upon it in the following terms.

    " It would be endleſs to notice all the errors of this
" preſumptuous pedant, whoſe dullneſs is equal to his
" impudence, his falſhood and malignity; and before he

Together we explored the stoic page   315

Of the Ligurian, stern tho' beardlefs fage !

NOTES.

To THEE fhe gave two piercing eyes,
A body——juft of Tydeus' fize. ·
   A judgment found, and clear ;
A mind with various fcience fraught,
A liberal foul, a thread bare coat,
   And forty pounds a year.

" makes a parade of greek quotations againft fuch a writer
" as Edwin *, he fhould at leaft learn latin ; but in this
" every merchant's clerk will detect him."

   * Our Ariftarchus is at " his old lunes," blundering
again. The only quotation I have made againft Edwin (to
ufe Mr. Parfons's elegant phrafe) is a latin, and not a greek
one—but 'tis lofs of time to talk to fuch naturals of
quotations. The morofoph Efte (Telegraph, April 28)
announced an Ode of Horace's as a compofition of Mr.
Parfons's, and Parfons himfelf undoubtedly miftook the verfe
alluded to, for a profe exclamation of my own !

Or traced the Aquinian thro' the Latine road,

And trembled at the lafhes he beftowed.

Together too, when Greece unlocked her ftores,

We roved in thought o'er Troy's devoted

        fhores ;   320

Or followed, while he fought his native foil,

" That old man eloquent" from toil to toil ;

Lingering with good Alcinoüs o'er the tale,

Till the eaft reddened, and the ftars grew pale.

NOTES.

To ME one eye not over good,
Two fides, that, to their coft, have ftood
    A ten years hectic cough ;
Aches, ftitches, all the numerous ills
That fwell the devilifh doctor's bills,
    And fweep poor mortals off.

A coat more bare than thine, a foul
That fpurns the croud's malign controul ;
    A fixed contempt of wrong ;
Spirits above affliction's power,
And fkill to charm the lonely hour
    With no inglorious fong.

So past our life ; till fate, feverely kind,   325
Tore us apart, and land and fea disjoined,
For many a year : now met, to part no more,
The afcendant Power, confeffed fo ftrong of yore,
Stronger by abfence, every thought controuls,
And knits in perfect unity our fouls.   330

    O IRELAND ! if the verfe that thus effays
To trace our lives " e'en from our boyifh
    days,"
Meet thy applaufe : the world befide may rail—
I care not——at the uninterefting tale :
I only feek, in language void of art,   335
To ope my breaft, and pour out all my heart ;
And boaftful of thy various worth, to tell,
How long we lov'd, and thou canft add, HOW
    WELL !

    Thou too, MY HOPPNER ! if my wifh availed,
Should'ft praife the ftrain that but for thee had
    failed :   340
Thou knowest, when Indolence poffeffed me all,
How oft I rouzed at thy infpiring call ;

Burft from the Syren's fafcinating power,

And gave the Mufe thou loveft, one studious
    hour.

  Proud of thy friendfhip, while the voice of
    fame   345

Purfues thy merits with a loud acclaim,

I fhare the triumph—not unpleafed to fee

Our kindred destinies ; for thou like me,

Waft thrown too foon on the world's dangerous
    tide,

To fink or fwim, as chance might best de-
    cide.   350

ME, all too weak to gain the distant land,

The waves had whelmed, but that an outstretched
    hand

Kindly upheld, when now with fear unnerved—

And still protects the life it then preferved.

THEE, powers untried, perhaps unfelt be-
    fore,   355

Enabled, tho' with pain, to reach the fhore,

While WEST stood by, the doubtful strife to
    view,
Nor lent a friendly arm to help thee through.

Nor ceafed the labour there : Hate, ill-fupprest,

Advantage took of thy ingenuous breast,   360

Where faving wifdom yet had plac'd no fcreen,

But every word, and every thought was feen,

To darken all thy life——'Tis past: more
    bright
Thro' the difparting gloom thou strikest the
    fight ;
While baffled malice hastes thy powers to
    own,   '   365
And wonders at the worth fo long unknown.

    I too, whofe voice no claims but truth's e'er
    moved,
Who long have feen thy merits, long have loved,
Yet loved in filence, lest the rout fhould fay
Too partial friendfhip tuned th' applaufive
    lay ;   370

Now, now that all confpire thy name to raife,
May join the fhout of unfufpeƈted praife.

Go then, fince the long struggle now is o'er,
And envy can obstruƈt thy fame no more ;
With ardent.hand thy magic toil purfue,   375
And pour frefh wonders on our raptured view.
One SUN is fet, one GLORIOUS SUN ; whofe
      rays
Long gladdened Britain with no common blaze :
O, may'ft THOU foon (for clouds begin to rife)
Affert his station in the eastern fkies,   380
Glow with his fires, and give the world to fee
Another REYNOLDS rifen, MY FRIEND, in
      THEE!

But whither roves the Mufe ?   I but defigned
To note the few whofe praife delights my mind ;
But friendfhip's power has drawn the verfe
      astray,   385
Wide from its aim, a long, but flowery way.
Yet one remains, ONE NAME for ever dear,
With whom, converfing many a happy year,

I marked with secret joy the opening bloom
Of Virtue, prescient of the fruits to come,   390
Truth, honour, rectitude——O while thy breast,
My BELGRAVE! of its every wish possest,
Swells with its recent transports, recent fears,
And tenderest titles strike, yet charm thy ears,
Say, wilt thou from thy feelings pause awhile, 395
To view my humble labours with a smile?
Thou wilt: for still 'tis thy delight to praise,
And still thy fond applause has crowned my lays.

  Here then I rest; soothed with the hope to
     prove
The approbation of " the few I love,"   400
Joined (for ambitious thoughts will sometimes
     rise)
Joined to th' endurance of the good and wise.
Thus happy—I can leave with tranquil breast
Fashion's loud praise to Laura and the rest,
Who rhyme and rattle, innocent of thought, 405
Nor know that nothing can proceed from nought.

Thus happy,—I can view unruffled, Miles,

Twift into fplay-foot doggrel all St. Giles.

Edwin fpin paragraphs with Vaughan's whole
    fkill,

Efte rapt in nonfenfe, gnaw his grey-goofe
    quill,   410

Merry in dithyrambics wail his wrongs,

And Wefton, foaming from Pope's odious
    fongs,

" Much-injured Wefton," vent in odes his grief,

And fly to Urban for a fhort relief.

IMITATIONS.

V. 410. Complures alios, doctos ego quos—
Prudens praetereo : quibus hæc fint qualiacunque
Arridere velim ; doliturus, fi placeant fpe
Deterius nostra. Demetri teque Tigelli,
Difcipularum inter jubeo plorare cathedras.

FINIS.